LORRAINE WILSON

I live in Wiltshire with my husband but love to travel and
have lived in four continents. From playing amidst Roman
ruins in Africa as a child to riding a Sultan's racehorse in the
Middle East as a teen, I've many experiences to draw on for
the stories I've been writing ever since I can remember. When
I'm not writing you'll find me listening to audiobooks while
I sew or design handbags, usually with a rescue terrier or two
curled up on my feet!

Revenge of a Chalet Girl

LORRAINE WILSON

A division of HarperCollins*Publishers*
www.harpercollins.co.uk

HarperImpulse an imprint of
HarperCollins*Publishers* Ltd
77–85 Fulham Palace Road
Hammersmith, London W6 8JB

www.harpercollins.co.uk

A Paperback Original 2014

First published in Great Britain in ebook format by HarperImpulse 2013

A catalogue record for this book is
available from the British Library

ISBN: 978-0-00-759172-5

Automatically produced by Atomik ePublisher from Easypress

*A big thank you to the team at HarperImpulse
but also special thanks to David, Lilian and
Doug for all your support. x*

CHAPTER ONE

No, no, no!

Amy's heart leapt wildly in her chest, pounding even harder than it had the time she'd tried a spinning class.

It has to be a different Josh Carter. It has to be!

Despite the crackling fire in the fireplace and cosy underfloor heating, Amy shivered.

"Are you okay there, Amy? Have you got those tree decorations? We're running out of time, especially if Scott and Holly have a clear run back from Geneva Airport," Sophie called out from the open-plan living area.

"Er, yes." Amy hastily put the bookings printout back by the telephone. That would teach her for being nosy. She picked up the cardboard box full of Christmas lights, glass icicles and shiny red baubles and walked into the room, taking it over to Sophie.

It's not my Josh, it can't be...

"Great." Sophie twisted her caramel-blonde hair up into a pony-tail and got up from the cowhide sofa to take the box from her. "I think we'll have enough now."

They both looked at the non-drop Christmas tree that soared up to the double-height ceiling in the corner opposite the fireplace. They'd already put two boxes' worth of decorations onto the tree and were fast running out of time before a minibus full of guests descended on them.

Tash and Amelia walked in, carrying four mugs of hot chocolate between them.

"Drink up, I've made them Irish." Tash winked at Amy, who attempted a weak smile, but it felt forced and unnatural; a reflection on how she was feeling – disconnected from her surroundings.

If it was *her* Josh Carter she needed the alcohol. And the chocolate. In fact, she'd need a shedload more of both…

"Thanks." Amy took her mug and tried to let the Michael Buble tracks playing softly in the background get her into the Christmas mood. Candles flickered on the windowsill and thick flakes of snow fell steadily outside, the sky so white it felt like they were immersed in the snow cloud.

It should be perfect. She had been looking forward to Christmas, even though she'd be working. There'd be parties, skiing and snow…

But now her mind was full of Josh, the thoughts had latched on, unshakeable. Memories of the last Christmas they'd shared together at his parents' house in Devon taunted her. Josh had saved up to buy her a silver hare brooch – he'd always joked she was like a hare, full of bounce and a bit wild. If anyone had suggested it was going to be the last time she'd celebrate it with him she'd have laughed.

Unthinkable.

She lifted the mug to her lips and swallowed a lump of pain down with the warm chocolate. The instant rush of sugar helped to take the sting away a little. She was used to swallowing down pain when it came to Josh. She'd had a lot of practice.

Christmas in Verbier had sounded such fun. Far better than going home to her parents and being asked if she'd met any nice boys yet, or when was she was going to settle to a "proper" job?

"Anyone know anything about the guests coming today?" She tried to sound casual, getting down on her knees on the cowskin rug to sort out the Christmas lights, testing the bulbs so she wouldn't have to look any of the girls in the eye. Sharing a dorm room meant they all knew each other pretty well.

Sometimes too well.

Tash was only too happy to share the gory details of her latest sexual conquests. How she got away with the things she got up to Amy didn't know. Luckily for Tash, Scott and Holly were great to work for and made it clear that what their staff got up to in their own time was their own business.

"I think it's a stag party." Sophie flopped back on the sofa with her mug and a packet of silver strands to untangle.

Amy and Amelia groaned, but Tash whistled. "Just think of the tips, girls."

"But what will they expect us to do for those tips?" Amelia pulled a face. "Don't you remember the time that stag group made us have a drinking competition to compete for our tips?"

"Hey, you might enjoy it. Don't knock it until you've tried it." Tash retorted. "Anyone'd think you were forty-six, not twenty-six."

"Where are they from? Oh crappitty, crap, crap…" Amy cursed as the plastic casing of one of the lights snapped in her fingers. She'd have to make sure that one went around the back of the tree.

"Who?" Tash stared at her curiously.

Really, that girl had the attention span of a gnat. Either that or she was being uncannily perceptive.

"The stag party of course." Amy's jaw clenched with the effort of trying to sound casual. Really, she wanted to grab hold of Sophie and shake the details out of her.

"Not sure," Sophie replied, sipping at her chocolate, fixing her hazel eyes on Amy. "Why?"

Why indeed?

Amy couldn't think of a reasonable answer. Not one she wanted to give, anyway. She shrugged, "Just wondering."

"Fancy your chances with one of them do you?" Tash asked. "Decided to stop being so choosy?"

"Leave her alone, Tash." Sophie got to her feet and came over to the box of decorations, emptying and sorting it with her usual efficiency. "Don't you want the field left clear for yourself?"

"There's plenty to go around and you've got to be generous at Christmas, haven't you?" Tash replied, grinning.

Amy fumbled with the lights, almost dropping them as she passed the string up to Amelia, now up on the stepladder next to the tree. Every muscle in Amy's body tensed and a familiar tight sensation had gripped her chest. She tried to reassure herself.

There were other Joshua Carters. There was absolutely no reason why it should be him. She's never heard him express an interest in skiing when they'd been together.

No, but you can bet he has the kind of friends who ski…who might invite him on their stag weekend.

She glanced at the clock on the wall, feeling positively twitchy. If the flight had arrived on time she'd find out soon enough. Her stomach lurched and when a wave of nausea washed over her, she dropped the end of the string of lights.

"What's up?" Amelia called down, flicking her straight blonde hair over her shoulder and fixing cool blue eyes on her.

"Sorry, I need the loo," Amy practically raced out of the room, ignoring the curious looks of the others and not waiting for a reply.

Instead of heading for the bathroom, she raced outside, desperate for fresh air, needing to breathe again. This hadn't happened to her for years. She'd never had panic attacks before, well, at least not before her life had imploded, leaving her crushed under the debris.

But she'd moved on from that bleak time, hadn't she? She had been depression-free for years, yet now it seemed to hover like a dark cloud on the horizon.

She focused on the view, on the dramatic plunge down into the valley, the alpine range soaring into the sky and the miles upon miles of pristine, powder snow. If she didn't anchor herself in the here and now she feared the past would catch up with her and sweep her away.

I should be over this…

The sunshine was warm on her face, despite the chilly wind. She inhaled the fresh mountain air, slowly deepening her breathing and trying to employ the special yoga techniques she'd learnt in class.

So many classes. So many attempts to keep busy, to keep moving so she wouldn't have to think. Now she'd been casually shoved off the precipice she'd painstakingly clawed her way up again. Just by seeing his name on a list.

Great progress Amy. You thought you were doing so well but look at you!

She persevered with the breathing and located her backbone.

Get it together.

She wouldn't let it get to her.

"It isn't Josh," she whispered fiercely to the mountains, as though speaking it aloud could make it true. If only she were free to go skiing this afternoon, that would've made her feel better. She needed a nice endorphin rush to flush the negative feelings out of her system.

And if it is Josh I'm going to give him hell. He won't get the satisfaction of seeing me looking defeated. He needs to see I'm over him.

Even if it isn't true.

The sun, now low in the sky, disappeared behind a lone darkgrey cloud and she shivered, wrapping her arms around her body.

I can do this.

Back in the chalet, she found Sophie and Amelia had gone into overdrive. The tree was decorated and it sparkled silver and red, reflecting the light of the candles they'd lit and placed around the room. All the decorations were tasteful. No gaudy tinsel here.

Yet a bit of her felt nostalgic for her tacky childhood Christmases. Mum would be bustling around at home now wearing her special Christmas apron, listening to carols on the radio and making mince pies. The house would be adorned with decorations they'd had for twenty or more years, including the angel Amy had made when she was six.

Amy grabbed her unfinished hot chocolate and gulped it down, trying hard to focus on all the skiing she'd be able to do this winter. Not to mention the parties. She'd be able to keep busy, so busy she wouldn't have to think.

"Could you go and check the cakes?" Tash asked, standing in her socks on the back of a dark leather chair and fastening what looked suspiciously like mistletoe to one of the beams. The pink streaks in her hair looked pretty cool in the candlelight. She'd been experimenting again.

"Okay." Amy turned back round again to go to the kitchen. "You know, I'm pretty sure Holly didn't ask for mistletoe."

"You've got to make your own opportunities, girl. You have so much to learn." Tash called out after her.

Hmm, maybe I should. It might be nice to meet someone.

Amy mentally pulled down the shutters on the past. It was time to move on; maybe a guy could help her do that.

As she pulled the trays from the oven she heard the crunch of tyres on the gravel outside, followed by voices. She quickly turned the first cake out onto a wire tray to cool and had picked up the second when the group spilled chaotically from the hallway into the kitchen.

"That smells amazing! I'm bloody starving, the food on the plane was crap." A large man with a thatch of blonde hair, the build of a rugby player and the face of an eager puppy advanced towards her, hand outstretched as though to grab the cake, tray and all.

The kitchen was so chaotic she couldn't properly scan the group for Josh.

She caught Holly's eye and Holly shrugged apologetically, surreptitiously raising her eyes to the ceiling.

"If you could all come this way there's a welcome drink for you by the fire," Holly announced to the group, attempting to shepherd them away from the kitchen. At the word "drink" they instantly obeyed. "Amy will bring the cakes through once they've cooled."

Amy anxiously trailed her gaze over every member of the group as the kitchen emptied. Even though, deep down, she was expecting Josh, it was still a shock when he turned to face her. She met his eyes – dark eyes, the colour of bitter coffee, fixed on her, mirroring her shock. His mouth opened as though he were going to speak, but he abruptly closed it again.

He was just the same, but not, somehow. A little broader in the chest perhaps, his complexion tanned and sun-kissed, his dark hair cropped closer to his head than she was used to. Stubble on his face too.

But still him. Oh God, it was still Josh.

The second cake tin slipped out of her hand and crashed to the slate floor, taking the oven mitt with it. It landed cake-side down. She scrambled down onto the floor to grab it, glad of an excuse not to have to speak to Josh, not to have to look. Stupidly, not thinking, she grabbed the tin with her now bare hand and cursed when it burnt her hand in the process.

"Ow, shit…shhhugar," she squeaked, catching Holly's eye and putting her hand to her mouth, her own eyes widening in horror. "Sorry, I'm so sorry."

She kept her eyes on the broken cake on the tiles, not daring to lock eyes with Josh again. She felt…she wasn't sure.

Overwhelmed might just about cover it.

"It doesn't matter. We've all done it." Holly replied briskly, ushering the last of the group, including Josh, firmly out of the kitchen. She then grabbed the mitt and retrieved the cake from the floor. "Run your hand under a cold tap. It's a shame they saw it happen, otherwise we could've brushed it off or cut the top off and iced it. The floor is clean after all."

"Really?" Amy went to the sink and turned on the cold tap, her cheeks hot. The pain helped somehow, it gave her something physical to focus on. Even the numbing cold water felt good. The numbness seemed to spread, creeping through her body and clinging to her mind, freezing her thoughts.

"Yes, you're not the first person to drop a cake and you won't be the last. That's why I've got a secret weapon stashed away where no one will find it." Holly went to a cupboard and pulled out Tupperware containers of dried lentils, retrieving a tin of luxury chocolate biscuits from behind them. "I have to hide the biscuits from Scott or he'd snaffle them. They'll do to go with the apple cake. Everyone likes a chocolate biscuit."

Holly then walked over to examine Amy's burn. "Are you okay?"

"I'm not, um, feeling that great. A bit sick ," Amy replied, gazing down at the sink. It wasn't a lie. She felt like she might throw up.

"Go and have a lie down then, that's an order," Holly said kindly. "We can manage the welcome bit and it's not your turn to do dinner tonight is it?"

"Er, thanks. If you're sure." Heat crept up Amy's neck. "I think I could do with a lie down."

A lie down. A stiff drink. And a fast car to get me out of here to Geneva Airport.

What the hell was she going to do now?

"I've missed you," Josh murmured in her ear, so close she could smell his aftershave and taste his skin. The recognition jolted her body as violently as an electric shock.

She moaned, pressing herself closer, willing him to touch her.

Thankfully she didn't have long to wait. Without any preamble, Josh kissed her as though they'd never been apart, his hands sliding up beneath her nightdress and squeezing her bottom.

His tongue probed into her mouth and she welcomed it enthusiastically, wanting him deeper and deeper.

She parted her legs, wet for him as she pressed hard up against him, wanting his hands and lips on her breasts, and his tongue between her legs. Wanting him with a ferocity that took her breath away.

Wanting him more than she'd ever wanted anything.

It felt so delicious, and utterly exquisite being with him again. It felt completely right. Like coming home.

Her body remembered his, remembered how well they fitted

together, like two pieces of a jigsaw puzzle. Hungrily, fervently she explored his firm flesh, her hands running up under the fabric of his t-shirt and snaking down to feel the hard bulge in his jeans.

"Josh," she gasped, wanting his clothes off, needing him to take her. "Josh, I need you."

"Amy," he whispered into her hair. "Amy, I…"

Then, with a sickening lurch she heard someone calling her name and she woke up, disoriented. She was not in Josh's arms after all but in the dorm room, in her bunk bed. Alone.

"Keep it down will you? Some of us are trying to sleep!" Amelia called out from the bunk below.

Blinking in confusion, Amy tried to adjust to cold reality as her dream faded. But her body throbbed as though he'd really been touching her and for a few moments she wanted to hold onto the sensation, wanted to stay in the dream where everything had magically been okay again.

"Not so fast," Tash said. In the dim light provided by the moonlight she was just visible in the bunk opposite. She'd turned on her side and was facing Amy. "So, who were you dreaming about?"

"Why? Oh no, was I talking in my sleep?" Amy groaned and shifted on her bunk. "Really?"

"Not exactly talking, I'd call it moaning." Sophie called out.

"And writhing, you were making the bed frame creak," Amelia added, clearly disgruntled. Amy wished she could melt away.

"Um, sorry." She wanted to shrink back under her bedclothes.

"Who's Josh?" Tash asked.

"Oh God, this is hideously embarrassing." Amy pulled the duvet up over her head.

"It's only sex," said Tash.

"Hmm." Amy winced beneath the covers. "I'm not really sure…"

Only sex? There was nothing "only" about sex with Josh. It had been fantastic.

It had meant something.

"There's nothing to be embarrassed about. Go on, dish the dirt.

Have you met someone? If so it's about time." Tash's voice was matter of fact, as though it were a perfectly normal conversation. Her attitude reassured Amy a little.

She poked her head out of the duvet. "I suppose I may as well tell you, I've got as much chance keeping a secret from you as from the Spanish Inquisition."

"Less chance," Sophie called out. "Go on, you can tell us. If you don't, you know Tash will only find out anyway."

"The Josh who arrived with the group today is, well, my ex…"

"Really?" Tash sounded very alert all of a sudden.

"Things didn't end well. He was the love of my life. I thought we'd get married and…" Amy's voice caught and she swallowed down the lump in her throat before continuing. "He dumped me, without any warning. We were getting on really well, there were no warning signs, nothing. It was a horrible shock and I um, didn't take it very well."

Big understatement.

She opened her mouth, but no words came out. How could she describe how depressed she'd felt when Josh had left for his job in Saudi? Then she'd got the news about Grandad's heart attack from mum. She'd been so close to him growing up and she'd not even got the chance to say goodbye.

No warnings. He'd just gone.

She'd slid into a horrific black hole the GP had diagnosed as clinical depression, once her mum had frogmarched her to the surgery. It was very common, the matter-of-fact doctor had briskly told her as she handed over a prescription for anti-depressants.

As though tablets could've brought either Josh or Grandad back.

As it was, the tablets seemed to increase the fog in her brain. She cried less but she no longer felt like herself.

She didn't feel up to talking about the long months of depression, the aborted teacher-training course and the worried parents. Would they even understand, or were they from the "pull yourself together" school of thought?

Anyway, she'd moved on from all that.

Josh didn't check on me once. He moved abroad and never looked back.

Stirrings of the old anger at his unrelenting silence simmered inside her, threatening to come to the boil. It hadn't helped that he hadn't been there to talk about Grandad. Josh had been her best friend as well as her boyfriend. They talked about everything. How did you just turn that off? Did it mean those years had never really meant anything?

Her eyes hurt from holding back the tears. Anger and pain mingling to create a deadly mixture that ate away at her insides.

For a moment, there was silence in the room, but Amy didn't trust herself to fill it.

"The bastard," Tash proclaimed. "So, it's time for revenge."

"Revenge? I don't know…" Amy wriggled uncomfortably in her bed. "I was thinking more along the lines of running away."

An indignant chorus filled the room.

"You can't run away. What are you, woman or wimp?" Tash asked.

Um, I'm a wimp probably. If I'm being honest.

"Woman," Amy replied reluctantly when it became obvious Tash expected an answer.

"This guy broke your heart, right?" Tash's sharp features looked fierce in the moonlight, like an alley cat about to pounce. "He trampled all over your emotions. Led you on and then dumped you."

"Well yes, I suppose so," Amy admitted, fighting the surging waves of emotion pressing against her eyelids.

I won't cry.

If she did, Tash would probably disown her for crimes against feminism. But could she ever forgive Josh for leaving her to deal with her first bereavement alone? For just switching their relationship off as though it meant nothing?

He had pulled the plug and watched the light and power fade out of her life and then he'd walked away.

That had felt like a bereavement too. That too had been a shock, the strike of lightning from a clear blue sky.

Amy curled up on the bunk, drawing her knees up against her chest.

"So, you get revenge and you get the upper hand." Tash cut into her thoughts, warming to her theme. "We can put chilli in his food and itching powder on his sheets."

"You'll get her fired," Amelia broke in, scornfully. "The best way to get revenge is to show him what he's missing and can never have again. Look gorgeous, flirt with his friends but be offhand and distant with him. Show him you are *so* over him. It will drive him insane. Trust me. And if he tries to get your attention, which take my word for it, he will, you blank him. That's the best revenge of all."

"That sounds kind of tempting. What do you think Sophie?" Amy asked.

"Do whatever you need to do to feel okay, sweetheart. You certainly can't hide in your room all Christmas and it's not fair on Scott and Holly to run away at their busiest time of the year." Sophie's voice was softer, kinder than the others. Amy trusted her advice.

"I suppose you're right," Amy sighed. Holly had been really good to her and why should Josh get to ruin her plans yet again? She could just imagine her parents' anxious expressions if they heard she'd thrown her job in, and even worse if they found out it'd been because of Josh.

She couldn't do that to them. She couldn't do it to herself.

"Getting revenge will make you feel much better, trust me," Tash said, yawning. And then maybe you won't dream about him and wake us all up."

"I'd certainly hate to be your enemy, Tash," Sophie laughed and turned over, making her bunk creak. "Now before we have the guy hung, drawn and quartered shall we all try and get some sleep?"

Amy listened to the rustling of bed clothes and tried to process everything – Josh turning up, the dream, the girls' advice... her head hurt with the effort of repressing the newly awoken emotions. Not to mention the carnal stirrings provoked by the dream and welcomed by her traitorous body.

She'd done such a good job of burying her desires, of picking herself up off the floor and getting on with life. It was gutting that by simply turning up, in one swift move Josh had brought all the balls she worked so hard to keep in the air crashing down to the ground, along with Tash's lemon drizzle cake.

She couldn't be a victim. Taking control of the situation was the way to go. He hadn't sought her out to speak to her since he'd arrived, had he? Was he worried she might make a scene? Perhaps he was horrified and was wondering how he would avoid her all holiday.

She'd give him a scene all right – but not the kind he might expect.

This time she'd be totally in control and she'd show him an Amy who was over him and doing damn well, thank you. Maybe she would flirt with his friends, and show him what he'd missed out on. She could wear that bikini Tash had talked her into buying to wear in the Jacuzzi.

Time to woman up and go on the offensive.

CHAPTER TWO

"Amy, can I have a word?" Josh hovered behind Amy in the kitchen. He still couldn't believe it was really her – Amy. In his chalet. After all the effort he'd made to try to get in touch and now she simply turned up.

And the timing couldn't be worse.

"Oh, hello Josh," Amy replied casually, almost off-hand. She even glanced at her watch.

This was awkward as hell, but he had to talk to her.

"I thought I ought to check you're okay with this?" He watched her, searching for the girl he'd once known. Once loved even...

"Okay with what?" She raised an eyebrow, drying her hands on a tea towel.

It's like that is it?

"Okay with me being here. You know, given our history."

"Of course it's okay." She shrugged. "Why wouldn't I be all right with it?"

That's me told then...

"No reason I suppose. If you're okay then that's...great. Only if you wanted, I could try to find some other accommodation? I'm not sure we'd manage to find somewhere for all four of us, but I could try..."

God this was hard.

"Don't be ridiculous." A spark of irritation flashed in her eyes, flaring into full-blown annoyance. "Why on earth would you do that? You'd end up paying twice. Holly and Scott wouldn't refund you at such short notice; no one would."

Why on earth? So it's just me this has thrown then, is it? Obviously.

His heart felt inexplicably heavy and his head pounded. The last thing he wanted tonight was another night out drinking. He needed a clear head.

How he was going to clear these thoughts from his mind was a headache in itself. Seeing Amy had rocked him to his foundations. He wanted to talk to her, to reconnect to the girl who'd been his best friend at university as well as his lover.

If only he'd known how rare that had been, instead of taking it for granted and assuming all relationships would be like that. How had he managed to lose touch with the person he was back then, not to mention his friends? None of the guys here with him this week had known him longer than a few years. Coping with the challenges of a new job and moving abroad had cut him off. He'd let it happen. And he'd paid dearly for his mistakes.

"Was that all you wanted?" Amy asked sharply. Where had her usual sunny smile and good nature gone? He missed the cheeky, smily girl he'd met in fresher's week. He hadn't seen a single genuine smile from her since he'd got here.

"Right, yes. I was wondering what time we're eating?"

"Seven o'clock. The same as last night." She turned her back to him, taking a pan drying from the draining board and plunging it into the soapy water again. Hadn't she already washed that?

"Great, well, I'll see you then." He forced a friendly smile to his face but quickly abandoned the attempt. After all, she wasn't even watching, so what was the point?

He shrugged and left the room. His muscles ached from the pistes that day; there'd been too much time at his desk lately. It'd been good to get out in the fresh air. But his head ached even more. He'd grab some ibuprofen; one of the guys must have something with them. If not then he'd ask one of the other chalet girls. Not Amy.

He knocked on Matt's door before entering his room.

"Got anything for a sore head?" He grimaced at Matt.

"Hair of the dog?" Matt glanced up at him from his iPod and gestured to the bottle of duty-free vodka on the bedside table.

Josh winced. "No, I was thinking more of headache tablets."

"I think there's some in my wash bag. Check the en suite." Matt took a swig from the bottle. "You're not turning into a lightweight on us, are you?"

"Hmm." Josh rummaged in the bathroom and took a couple of tablets. "Maybe we could give the bars a miss tonight?"

"And miss S Lodge? Weren't we going there tonight?"

"STD lodge more like. Isn't that what the seasonnaires call it?" Josh snorted. He shook his head and instantly regretted it. Christ that hurt. "We could just hang out here."

"We could give the jacuzzi a go." Matt's eyes gleamed. "And we can get the chalet girls to join us. Great thinking mate."

"Well, er…" Josh frowned. This was going to be difficult. He didn't need the added complications. But then…Amy didn't seem to give a stuff. "Maybe."

It would be better than giving his liver another battering.

Who are you trying to kid?

"Think they'd be up for a bit of fun?" Matt took another slug of vodka. "I like the look of that little blonde with the green eyes and the heart-shaped face, Amy I think her name is."

Ice trickled down Josh's spine. "I'm sure there are rules about them dating guests." Josh frowned.

"Rules are made to be broken." Matt winked back.

Josh watched Matt at dinner and saw his eyes flicker over Amy's breasts when she bought their starters to the table.

He wanted to throttle him.

"These look nice," Josh gestured towards the goat's cheese tart-lets. "Did you make them yourself?"

"I helped to make them, yes." She avoided his eye and slid into her seat.

He took a sip of water, but before he'd even picked up his cutlery Amy leapt out of her seat and darted towards him, eyes wide with anxiety.

"I'm sorry, I've given you the wrong plate." She snatched his tartlet away before he had time to pick up his cutlery. "This one's mine, it's er…gluten-free pastry. Have this one instead."

She put her own plate in front of him.

"You're gluten-intolerant? Since when?" he asked, the words escaping from his mouth before he could stop them.

Everyone stared, expressions ranging from blank to curious. He wondered if anyone knew they'd dated. He'd not said anything to the guys because, well, it was private stuff. Had Amy told the other chalet girls?

Probably. Girls talked about that stuff, didn't they?

"It's just I'm sure I saw you eat a croissant at breakfast," he added.

Thank God he'd dodged that bullet! At least he hoped he had. He could really do without his relationship with Amy getting out. He'd never hear the end of it.

"That was a…er…special croissant," Amy said tersely, picking at the tartlet she'd taken from him and pushing it around the plate. "It was made with gluten-free flour."

He watched her; his own appetite had vanished too, despite the day's skiing. Mountain air usually made him ravenous. He wanted to get Amy by herself. He needed to talk to her.

"Aren't you going to eat it?" he asked her, ignoring a curious gaze from Matt.

"I'm not very hungry." She grabbed her water glass and glugged down the contacts, her face crimson as she refused to look at him.

Curious.

"Excuse me while I check on the main course." She pushed her chair back and sprang up, walking briskly to the kitchen.

He ignored the impulse to get up and follow her, feeling not only Matt's eyes on him but Paul's and Mark's too.

He sighed.

Of all the chalets in all the world why did you have to turn up in mine?

Amy opened the freezer door and plunged her face in, welcoming the chilled air.

Tash came into the kitchen behind her. "Why on earth did you switch the plates? Are you mad?"

"He's allergic to chilli." Amy leant back against the freezer. "I only remembered at the last minute."

Lying to Tash was much easier than admitting she'd decided it was too childish and she didn't want to go through with it.

"Hmm, I spose that might've been going too far." Tash shrugged. "But remember, this is the guy who hurt you so much you were thinking of running away from Switzerland. You don't have to tell me all the details, but I can tell he really hurt you. You can't let that go."

"I know, you were only trying to help." Amy smiled weakly and walked to the sink to fill another glass of water. "Just how much chilli did you put in that tartlet? I only had a tiny bit of it and now it feels like my mouth's on fire."

"I put a fair bit in." Tash admitted.

Amelia and Sophie came into the kitchen, carrying the empty starter plates.

Sophie took one look at Amy's face. "The chilli? I thought I talked you out of that? At least you changed your mind at the last minute I suppose."

Amy nodded miserably.

"Are you glad you didn't go through with it?" Sophie stacked the plates in the dishwasher.

"Mmm." Amy shrugged and leant back against the counter

with a sigh.

"My method of revenge is much better." Amelia said, lips pursed. "Make him see what he's missing."

"The guys are staying in this evening. Matt asked if we could show them how to work the jacuzzi," Tash said, winking.

"You just press the button, it's not exactly difficult," Amy folded her arms across her chest, not liking where this was going one bit.

Amelia stared at her like she was nuts. "You can use this to get the upper hand. Put on that bikini you bought the other day. Flirt with Matt. I think he fancies you. That will wind Josh up and you won't get into trouble."

"Maybe." Amy sipped at her water, the heat in her mouth thankfully subsiding to something resembling a normal temperature. It was tempting; there'd been something close to pity in his eyes when he'd asked her if she was okay with him being here.

Patronising git.

Of course she wasn't okay but she'd die rather than tell him that.

"Or you could cut out the middle man and flirt with Josh instead?" Tash suggested, raising her eyebrow as she ladled servings of casserole into the dinner plates. "Shag him and dump him, I say."

Amy snorted.

"I saw something in my magazine about sex with exes, you know," Amelia said. "Scientists have carried out some kind of study about it, proving it helps you come to terms with the end of the relationship."

Amy wished Tash hadn't said anything; as if it hadn't been hard enough to keep the memories of sex with Josh at bay. The spark of desire inside her had flared into flame at the suggestion, as though given permission to do the unthinkable.

"Erm, I don't know if that's a good idea," Amy replied, trying to claw back control over the raging emotions now pressing their case loudly and vociferously, bombarding her with images of Josh on top of her, his hands running all over her body, making love to her in a way that made her bones melt. No one had made love to her like that since.

Her body craved the experience again.

Remember what he did. He cut you off cold and abandoned you when you needed him most. He didn't care. Maybe if he'd stayed, or asked you to go with him, maybe it could've been different...

Amy crushed the hateful "what-ifs". It was pointless to think like that. It didn't help anything. It certainly didn't help her.

"As long as the 'L' word isn't mentioned and no one drops the GBT bomb it's supposed to be fine. Positively good for you, in fact," Amelia said.

"The GBT bomb?" Amy briefly wondered if it was some kind of new sexual fad that'd passed her by.

"Getting Back Together." Amelia took a couple of plates and together they carried the main course in.

Amy glanced at Tash suspiciously. Had she done something to Josh's main course as well? But the plates were all mixed up, so she couldn't have done. She couldn't meet his eye as she dished out the food and took her seat. But she felt his gaze on her, as palpable as if he were stroking her body. Her skin prickled and she grew hot again but this time for an entirely different reason.

She pushed her food around the plate, not remotely hungry. Every muscle felt tense and on high alert. Her thoughts were stuck on a permanent Josh loop, torturing her over and over with memories of making love to him and then the sheer misery of losing him. He'd left her to go through that alone.

I need to remember how much he hurt me. I must remember...

She turned to Matt, forcing a smile to her face. "So, are you guys going out this evening?"

"We thought we'd stay in tonight." Matt leant closer, his eyes gleaming with sudden interest. "Would you like to show us how to use the jacuzzi?"

Amy willed herself not to move away. It felt weirdly disloyal to Josh to be flirting with Matt, but that was crazy. Anyway, Josh had done the ultimate in disloyalty...

"Sure, why not? We'll come and join you once we've cleared up." She aimed for breezy but thought her voice sounded squeaky, like a panicked mouse.

Only when it was time to clear the table did she catch Josh's eye and when she did, she flinched. He glared at her, eyes dark and when she attempted a smile to break the tension he didn't return the gesture.

This was totally pants.

She carried the plates back into the kitchen, tears stinging the backs of her eyelids as she fought to keep them from escaping. What right had Josh to be angry with *her*? She was the innocent one in all this and she had the right to flirt or sleep with whom-ever she wanted.

Angrily, she stacked the plates, barely aware of the girls around her. She wanted to hurt Josh at that moment, really hurt him. Revenge might be best served cold but her revenge was going to be hot, red-hot. She'd make him see what he'd been missing.

Standing outside on the chilly terrace, protected from the icy air and the snow by only a white waffle robe and slippers, her red-hot rage had cooled a little. Goosebumps crept over her flesh as the others whooped and ran to the hot tub. Tash pressed the button to start it up and leapt in. She hadn't even bothered with a robe, just a skimpy black bikini, and for a second Amy wondered if she'd ever be so confident as to not care at all about how she looked.

She slipped the waffle gown from her shoulders, the soft cotton brushing her sensitised skin. Glancing down, she was horribly aware of her nipples stiffening with the cold and pressing hard against the fabric of her silver bikini. She couldn't meet Josh's eyes or bear his glare. She bristled; it was hardly as if she'd done anything wrong.

Out of the corner of her eye she noticed Matt's appreciative gaze resting on her body. Despite the cold a flush crept up her neck and she stared hard at the decking, keeping her slippers on until she got to the tub. No way was she running over the snow like Tash had done.

She stepped down into the hot water of the tub trying not to feel self-conscious, which was counter-productive. The silver fabric protecting her modesty felt flimsy and insubstantial. Matt reached out a hand to help her down and she took it, accepting his help and stirred by the appreciative gleam in his eye and his cheeky grin. So, it'd been a good move being talked into buying the silver bikini. She'd not thought to pack a swimsuit. She'd been thinking about keeping warm when she did her packing back in England.

The bikini was a little smaller than she'd realised, though, and the cold air had had a rather unfortunate effect on her nipples – they poked prominently through the flimsy fabric.

How embarrassing.

For a brief moment she wondered if she wanted to take things further with Matt. He seemed…nice enough. His chest was broad and muscly, thick dark hair curled down his chest to beneath the waistband of his trunks.

As Amy sank into the warm water Matt rested a hand on her back, resting lightly over her bikini fastening.

"Don't grope the girl," Josh barked, descending rapidly after Matt, his face dark as thunder as he squeezed in between Sophie and Amy.

Hmm, interesting…

"Amy doesn't mind, do you Amy?" Matt said, shooting Josh a curious, half-amused look.

"Er, no…it's fine." Amy shrugged awkwardly, shrinking back onto the underwater shelf that served as a seat in the hot tub.

Tash was chatting up the other two guys on the other side of the hot tub. Amy couldn't remember their names; she'd been a bit…preoccupied.

She couldn't concentrate, even though her body felt on high alert and her heart beat hard in her chest.

Thud. Thud. Thud.

They had all squeezed up to make room, fitting eight in was tight. Josh's thigh pressed hard against her on one side and Matt's thigh on the other, but it was Josh's leg which sent darts of pleasure zinging around her body, like she'd received a shot of adrenalin.

This felt too intimate, too stressful. How could Tash and Amelia chat and flirt as though it were perfectly normal to strip after dinner and climb into what was in effect a giant bath? With strangers too.

Her skin prickled, nipples still hard despite the warmth of the water. Steam rose into the air, evaporating as hot met cold.

And this is supposed to be relaxing? Huh!

All she could think about was Josh's thigh pressed up against hers. Erotic images flashed through her mind, unexpected and X-rated.

If they were alone in this tub, how easy it would be to surreptitiously untie the ties of her bikini bottoms and slip onto Josh's lap. To slowly grind against him until he slid inside her…

The first time they'd made love had been outdoors. Did Josh remember it as well as she did? He had been adamant their first time wouldn't be in the back of his battered MG Metro so they'd driven out into the country and climbed a fence into a field. She could almost inhale the fresh night air of that evening, feel the blades of grass beneath her bare bottom, and feel Josh moving inside her.

She glanced sideways at him and found he was looking at her, as though drawn to her by the strength of her fantasies and erotic memories. His eyes were dark, dilated with desire, melting and tempting her. Yet there was still the distance between them that had broken her heart the day he'd ended their relationship. As though he wanted her but had already decided he wasn't going to have her.

He'd always been about doing the right thing.

Maybe I should show him Amelia's magazine article.

Where had this come from? How had rage morphed into a

ferocious desire to make love to him?

Casually she pressed her thigh a little harder against his, wondering if the bubbles could adequately hide everything that happened beneath the surface of the water.

"How have you been Amy?" Josh whispered, beneath the sound level of the others' voices. The noise of the jacuzzi helped to cover the sound of their voices.

"Um, okay," she whispered back, enjoying the intimacy that the whispering brought them. This was their little world, right here. "And you?"

He hadn't moved his thigh away and its presence disturbed her, sending messages cartwheeling through her body.

"I'm, yes…I'm great." His smile didn't quite reach his eyes. It wasn't his easy-going grin of old that she'd loved so much. Just one smile from Josh had been all she ever needed to raise her spirits.

She thought he looked a little…sad. As they stared she felt the barriers between them dissolving and a glimmer of their old connection resurfaced temporarily.

"Amy, why aren't you teaching?" he asked and Amy's stomach lurched. "Are you taking a year off or something?"

The one question she couldn't bear to answer. How on earth could she tell him? It was all much too late.

"No, I…" Amy's voice refused to obey her, the words catching in her throat. The sense of shame morphed into anger.

It might've been different if you'd been there. If you'd bothered to hang around or maybe if you'd just stayed in touch and been there to listen…maybe I wouldn't have fallen into that black hole.

Yet despite the anger she couldn't bring herself to shift away from his thigh. Desire flared through her, between her thighs, deep inside and in her tingling nipples. The dichotomy of anger and desire wound her even tighter and fear she might detonate any minute pulsed through her body.

There'd be carnage, she was sure of it.

"I don't teach, I um, never actually did the teacher training in the end. I temped instead. And I travelled a little. Then I heard about working the season out here, that they wanted English speakers and you could have about all the skiing you wanted. So I ended up here." Her voice tailed off at the confused frown on Josh's face.

Feeling that she'd disappointed him hurt, which in turn angered her.

How can I be feeling like this? It's ridiculous; he's the one who bloody well disappointed me, big time!

Tash, Paul and Mark had leapt out of the tub and were rolling in the snow, shrieking loudly and providing a welcome distraction. At least Tash was having a good time. She was never happier than when two guys were vying for her attention.

Amy looked down at the water, at the bubbles rising to the surface and evaporating. This was supposed to be relaxing? She felt as jumpy as a kangaroo on steroids. She fidgeted away from Josh, which left her with nowhere to go but closer to Matt. Her thigh pressed up against his hairy leg.

He turned to her and grinned, breaking off his conversation with Amelia. "Hi there. Stop chatting up the chalet girls, Josh."

"I was only talking to her," Josh's tone was mild but she recognised the expression on his face.

Josh was pissed off. Very pissed off.

"Well you're already taken mate. Have a bit of pity for your single friends." Matt lightly stroked Amy's thigh beneath the surface of the water.

Amy couldn't move, whether she was immobilised from the news that Josh was taken or Matt's advances she wasn't sure. She didn't know how to handle either.

"Oh." The breath caught in Amy's chest as she turned her head to see Josh's face. "You are?"

She was barely aware of Matt's hand continuing to stroke her leg, she cared only about what Josh would say next.

Of course he has a girlfriend.

The voice in her head was scornful.

"Well he is the stag." Matt laughed. "And I don't think his fiancée would take kindly to him chatting up the chalet girls. No offence."

CHAPTER THREE

Josh's eyes sought hers, staring hard, as though trying to communicate without words, his mouth set in a grim line. But what was he trying to say? And really what could he say? She shifted away from him, which meant she was pressed even harder against Matt.

"Oh I see, I didn't think." Amy blinked hard to stop the tears from falling. Why hadn't it occurred to her that Josh might be the stag? But then hadn't she deliberately avoided asking which of the group was getting married? Hadn't she really feared this, deep down?

What does it matter? You weren't really thinking about getting back together with him were you? He dumped you, cut you off without a word, let you go through hell without giving a toss what might be happening to you…

She turned to Matt, her back to Josh, feeling like her insides had turned to lead. "So Matt, you don't have a girlfriend or fiancée hidden away somewhere then?"

She hoped Josh could read the subtext.

Why on earth didn't you tell me you're getting married?

Matt grinned, eyes gleaming. "Me? No, I'm free to be all yours, if you want me."

She raised an eyebrow, ignoring a derisive snort from Josh behind her. "Does that usually work as a chat up line?"

Matt shrugged "Well, I don't like to brag but…okay not often. Why don't you take pity on me and give me a kiss?"

Amy sensed Josh's hostility behind her. What did he care? He was getting married wasn't he? It was none of his business who she kissed. Matt's interest was both flattering and reassuring.

Ignoring the thumping of her heart she leant forward. Matt's green eyes widened with delighted surprise, but he swooped in before she could reconsider.

His warm lips felt nice, she supposed. It was a…good-ish kiss. But she felt detached from it, like an observer. She went through the motions but her heart wasn't in it. All her awareness was focused on Josh getting out of the tub behind her. She heard the splash and couldn't concentrate on the kiss. Tears still burned in her eyes and she kept them tightly shut, squeezing them hard and trying to ignore the beating drum of the news.

Josh is getting married. Married. Married! It can't be true. This isn't what was meant to happen.

And this wasn't fair to Matt. His hands had edged up from her thigh. She had to act quickly. Before they could creep further towards her breasts she edged away.

"Sorry, I think I had a bit too much wine at dinner," she said, wondering if he'd noticed she'd barely touched her glass. If so, he was too polite to say so. "I made a… mistake, I shouldn't have…"

Matt put both his hands up, palms facing her. "Hey, no need to apologise, feel free to make your mistakes with me anytime. I'm always glad to be of service."

She smiled despite the wave of misery threatening to swamp her. He was a nice guy; if it hadn't been for Josh, well maybe…but at the moment it wasn't fair for her to get involved with anyone.

Not while her heart was so firmly trapped in the past. It wasn't right.

Kissing Matt had been like putting a sticking plaster on a broken leg – entirely inappropriate, not to mention inadequate.

Until tonight, she hadn't even realised she was holding out

hope she and Josh might be able to resurrect things. Hoping for a last-minute reprieve. As though Josh was going to confess he'd been in love with her all along, pining for her and cursing himself for making the mistake of a lifetime.

As if.

She had to get real. The past was dead and buried. It was time to stop faffing about with her life, waiting for someone to make everything okay again.

She stumbled out of the jacuzzi, scalding tears burning her eyes. Somehow she managed to locate her discarded gown and slippers and get back into the chalet.

Josh is getting married, married! Who is she? This woman who is so much more perfect for him than me?

She slipped the gown on, not bothering to do it up, and it hung loosely around her dripping body. Eyes blinded by tears, she stared at the ground as she stumbled inside, making her way towards the dorm room. She didn't switch the corridor light on, not wanting anyone to see her tears.

When she collided with someone she knew it was him; even though it was dark, her body seemed to recognise him. In the shock of sudden impact, flesh meeting flesh, she froze, unable to pull away. She reached her hand out to his still-wet chest, his flesh warmer than her cold trembling fingers.

"Josh?" Her voice trembled.

Josh felt like someone had hit the pause button on his life. Of all the bloody rotten luck, this had to happen now, of all times! To feel Amy's pert little breasts bumping against his chest and her hand reaching out for him just as he'd been thinking about her was a cruel joke. His resistance felt low.

Dangerously low.

It's too late.

With great effort he stepped back. "Excuse me."

He hated that his voice sounded stiff, not like him at all. As though he were addressing a total stranger. He cleared his throat. Watching her kissing Matt had been torture. She'd done it to hurt him, he was sure of it, or was that just his wishful thinking, to imagine she might still feel something for him?

Not that it mattered either way because he couldn't do anything about it. Couldn't and wouldn't. No matter how tempting it was to take hold of her right now and rip that silver bikini from her body before ravishing her right here in the hallway.

God, she might as well have set out to deliberately hurt him. This was hell. Something like a groan emanated from his throat.

"Are you okay?" Amy whispered.

"Yes," Josh lied. "I'd better let you get to your room."

He stood back against the wall, trying to make as much room as possible, not daring to trust what he might do if her breasts grazed his chest again. The swell of longing for her made his lungs feel like they were going to burst.

I have to do the right thing. However hard it is.

Didn't he always? Hadn't it been instilled in him to find the right path in life and stick to it regardless? And doing the right thing by a woman was a given, an absolute.

Amy hadn't moved yet. Her breathing was audible in the quiet hallway. In the distance he could hear the other girls shrieking and plenty of male laughter as some kind of game got underway. At least someone was a having a good time on his stag party.

Remember Juliet. You've made a commitment to her and you have to stick to it.

But this really was the cruellest test.

Amy tentatively reached out a hand to touch his arm and he jumped as though a bolt of electricity had shot through him. He stepped rapidly away from her. It took all his effort not to touch back, not to kiss her like that bastard Matt had done. He wanted her so much it felt like a physical need.

He sighed wearily. "I can't Amy, I can't."

He turned and walked back down the corridor to his room,

trying to quash his fear that she might be crying. He'd only want to take her in his arms if she was and who knew what might happen if he did that?

Actually he had a very good idea what might happen if he did that. Hadn't he been dreaming about it ever since he'd arrived and found Amy here?

He'd been going back to the jacuzzi to find a way of breaking up what was happening between Matt and Amy, even if he had to physically drag Matt back to his room. Matt could never make a girl like Amy happy and he was just after a quick grope and a shag if he could push his luck.

Amy deserved more than that. So much more.

He hauled himself into his room, engulfed by a horrible sense of déjà vu as he sat wearily on the bed, not caring that his trunks were wet and soaking through the sheets. He could still sense her presence in the corridor. She was so very temptingly close.

Juliet, think of Juliet.

He collapsed back on the bed, staring up at the dark ceiling. Usually he was confident his moral compass was in good working order but right now it pointed in only one direction – towards Amy.

He'd have to find a way of overcoming this. He had to do the right thing by Juliet; he'd made a commitment. They were getting married in just over a week. Everything had been arranged and Juliet would be on her way to Verbier soon, after her hen weekend in Ibiza. Maybe once Juliet was here it would help him focus?

He cursed and squeezed his eyes shut, but all he could see was Amy in her silver bikini. She was looking more womanly since university and the extra curves suited her. Why wasn't she teaching though? Her answer troubled him. Something had clearly gone wrong, but what?

He'd been so sure he was doing the right thing, setting Amy free to follow her dreams. And once he'd got to Saudi and seen the kind of enclosed life on a compound she'd have been confined to he was sure of it. They could only have gone together if they'd married and his dad had been so persuasive… they were too young and Amy wouldn't have been able to start her teacher training; she'd have ended up resenting him.

I think that ship's already sailed.

He grimaced. All those arguments had seemed so reasonable. He'd trotted them out so many times he'd learnt to crush his longing for her. Of course he'd missed her. There was a part of him that wanted her with him in Saudi and sod the consequences. But that was selfish and you had to make decisions with your head, not your heart. Didn't you?

He looked up, but there was no answer from the dark ceiling. Not that he really believed his dad was up there, somewhere, listening and about to dispense ghostly wisdom. No, this time he was very much on his own. Ridiculously, the only person he wanted to talk to was the one person he couldn't – Amy.

She was just the other side of that door and he couldn't go to her. Wasn't that the funniest thing? Yep, practically hysterical. It certainly made him want to howl.

Of course he didn't, instead he forced himself to get up off the bed and head into the en-suite to shower. Then he'd pick up a book and hope the words could drive the thoughts from his mind until he was so tired he'd fall asleep. A dreamless sleep. He couldn't bear to dream of Amy again.

After all, he'd done this before. He knew how to make himself do things he didn't want to, it was part of life, part of growing up. Crushing his desires was almost second nature.

And this was the biggest test of all.

Rejected didn't come close to covering how Amy was feeling. She lay on her bunk, staring at the ceiling and feeling glad it wasn't her turn to cook tonight. Every word Josh had said to her since he arrived seemed to be running a continuous loop in her head and she couldn't find a pause button.

Some things were hard to stomach. Josh had actually flinched when she'd reached out to him. Flinched, as though she had a contagious disease and would infect him just by touch. A fresh wave of humiliation swept through her as she gazed miserably up at a lone cobweb in the corner of the ceiling.

Spending the day on the slopes hadn't been the usual effective distraction. Simultaneous hope and dread that she might run into Josh had plagued her and the blue skies and sunshine failed to impact her mood.

Why on earth do I want to see him? Am I a glutton for punishment?

But she did; she wanted to see him even if it hurt, even though it meant not only opening up the wounds but emptying an entire salt cellar over them.

I still can't believe he's getting married. I wonder what she's like...

"Are you ready to talk about it yet?" Tash's voice from the opposite top bunk broke through Amy's thoughts.

Amy turned over in her bunk to glance at Tash. She lay on her front, propped up by the elbows, an issue of a German fashion magazine spread out on the pillow in front of her. It was worrying that she hadn't even heard Tash come into the room.

"It's too…humiliating," Amy groaned. "I really, really made an idiot of myself."

"I doubt it," Tash said cheerfully. "It was a good move kissing Matt. You should've seen Josh's face. I thought he might fly at Matt – he certainly wanted to."

Something flickered inside Amy, the faintest spark of hope desperately seeking oxygen. She fought the impulse to fantasise and give that hope fuel.

Josh doesn't want you. He's getting married. You have to walk away.

"That wasn't what I was talking about." Amy turned over and buried her head into her pillow. Really she wanted to crawl under the duvet, pull it up over her head and never come out.

Ever.

The humiliation still tormented her to such a degree it felt like a physical presence in her chest, constricting her breathing and choking her. Josh had been oh, *so* close to her. She'd practically been able to feel the warmth from his body and his heart beating beneath her fingertips.

Her body had responded with a physical recognition and she'd reached out without thinking. Without even knowing what she was asking for.

I just wanted to make contact, but he couldn't even let me have that.

"So, what were you talking about then? Tell Tash, you know it's for the best," Tash proclaimed loudly.

Amy brought her head up from the pillow, she had to stop remembering how it felt, being so close to Josh. Nothing was going to happen. It couldn't happen, so she needed to get over it. End of.

"I sort of, well, touched him. Josh I mean," Amy said, finding it hard to explain the intimacy and strangeness of their corridor encounter.

"You touched him?" Tash shrieked with laughter.

"Ssh," Amy hissed. "Everyone will hear you."

"So, where did you touch him?" Tash asked, smirking.

"Just on his chest, and I didn't really mean to. God, you have got such a dirty mind." Amy rolled her eyes.

"So what's the big deal?" Tash shrugged.

"He flinched away from me like…like I disgusted him." Amy struggled to hold the tears back. A few escaped and rolled down the side of her face onto the pillowcase.

"You want him back? Because I thought you wanted revenge. Getting him back is a whole different set of advice. Maybe I should hold off on the itching powder then?" Tash asked.

"Tash, I told you I didn't want to do that stuff!" Amy exclaimed.

"I'm joking."

"Hilarious." Amy sat up on her bunk, draping her legs over the edge and swinging them to and fro. It must be so easy to be like Tash, to be so certain of everything and not give a damn what anyone thought.

"Well, I'm not sure what I wanted or want now to be honest, maybe a bit of both. I'm not sure it could even work out, us being a couple."

She wiped the rogue tears away with the back of her hand.

Imagine if they were back together. She'd torment herself wondering if he was about to pull the rug out from underneath her feet again, bringing her life crashing down around her.

After all, he'd done it once before. So how could she ever be sure he wouldn't do it again? There was only one answer to that.

She couldn't.

"But you want him to want you, regardless, don't you?" Tash's intelligent eyes focused on her. She was wasted as a chalet girl, she should work as an interrogator. She had ways and means of winkling information out of you.

"Of course." Amy shrugged ruefully. "No one likes being rejected. You know I still can't believe he's getting married."

"Because he's still so young, you mean?" Tash said.

No, because he should've married me.

"I know this is going to sound silly but you've heard those people who say 'I knew I was going to marry him the moment I saw him'? Well, I was one of them. Don't laugh! I really believed it." Amy hesitated.

"Really?" Tash asked, eyeing her quizzically.

"Yes." Amy nodded. When she'd met Josh that day in the university bar, her heart had gone into free-fall. "Shows how wrong I was, eh? He's marrying someone else."

"But you didn't carry on believing that after you broke up, surely?"

Amy hesitated. "I suppose, deep down, I thought maybe one day we'd get back together and magically we'd get over everything that happened and…I so need to get over myself, don't I?"

"You need to get over him you mean." Tash threw her a packet of facial wipes. "Now clean your face up, I've got some serum we can put under your eyes to bring down the puffiness and then I can do your make-up for you if you like. Look fabulous and adopt the 'fuck-you' attitude."

"Like you do, you mean?" Amy took one of the wipes and started on her eyes. Just wiping away the tears felt like a good start.

No more tears.

Amy could practically feel her spine stiffening. Tash was right, she couldn't hide away forever and why should she have to? This was her Christmas too and she had a job to do.

"It works for me." Tash shrugged. "Do you have any better ideas?"

CHAPTER FOUR

Josh knew he looked a wreck. No sleep and a monumental hangover could do that to you. The book hadn't worked. In the end he'd turned to Matt's bottle of duty-free vodka in a futile attempt to keep the demons at bay.

Because, boy, had they done a good job tormenting him ever since he'd locked eyes on Amy again. They'd really gone on the offensive after she'd reached out to him in the hallway. He knew that just one step closer, one touch, one word more and they'd have ended up in bed together.

I've done the right thing. Of course I have.

He was so not the guy to have a meaningless fling on his stag weekend.

As if sex could ever be just a meaningless fling with Amy.

As if summoned by his thoughts of her Amy breezed into the living room, her hair glossy, curls bouncing as she walked. Her skin looked flawless. In fact she looked beautiful. Amazing.

She turned in his direction and her gaze passed over him, hard as flint and as freezing cold as the sub-zero temperatures outside.

It took all his self-control to remain impassive. His jaw tightened with the effort and his fingers itched to reach out and touch her, to recall her to him. Because she felt miles away.

This was hell. Absolute hell.

If only I'd found her when I came back to England. Things might've been different.

But they weren't and it was utterly useless to think like that. He was marrying Juliet and that was that. He'd made his proverbial bed and now he had to lie in it. With Juliet.

Just thinking of beds made him remember Amy lying in his bed at uni, her naked limbs tangled with his as she giggled. She was always giggling about something back then and her uncomplicated joy and relentless energy had been one of the things he loved about her.

He glanced over to where she was gathering placemats and cutlery and laying the table with quiet concentration, her face blank. No smile in sight, never mind a giggle.

He badly wanted to make her laugh again, to find out what had gone wrong for her. Her explanation about temping didn't add up; she'd been so excited about teacher training.

He walked over to the table. "Would you like some help?"

"That's okay thanks," she replied stiffly, her gaze lowering to the fork she held, turning it over as though inspecting it for smears. "I'm paid to do this and it's your holiday, remember?"

The words felt loaded, like missiles designed to wound.

Yes, you're on your stag weekend, remember?

"I don't mind." He picked up some of the mats and began putting them in place around the table before she could argue with him.

"So, you're getting married." Amy's voice sounded cold but he noticed her fingers trembled and she dropped the napkins.

"Er, yes." He grabbed them for her and put them on to the table. What should he do? Ignore the trembling and not mention it? Was that the kindest thing to do?

Evidence that she wasn't as cool as she pretended to be cheered him up, but also worried him.

"So, are your parents coming over for the wedding? Where will they be staying?" she asked brightly. "It will be really nice to see them again."

All the temporary positivity drained from him as quickly as though he were a bath and Amy had pulled the plug. He opened his mouth to speak but it felt disconnected from his brain.

She doesn't know.

"You haven't heard then? I did try to let you know. I had thought you might come…" His voice choked up and he couldn't say the word, it still felt too raw.

"I haven't heard what?" She whispered, her eyes widening with anxiety. She stepped closer. "What's wrong?"

Her features softened and he glimpsed the Amy he remembered, the best friend and confidante. The Amy he missed.

"I'm afraid they both passed away, Amy, a year ago, in a motorway pile up. Dad died at the scene of the accident and Mum two days later in hospital." It was odd how easily the words tripped off his tongue. He still felt as detached from those words as he had every other time he'd had to deliver the news to friends and relatives. As though a part of him still refused to believe it ever happened.

"Oh." Her face blanched white as snow and she swayed.

He stepped forward to hold her and guided her to a chair to sit down. "I'm sorry to have to give you the bad news."

"I'm so, so sorry Josh, that's awful, I know how close you were to them."

Josh just about managed to nod in acknowledgement, feeling close to coming undone. Hearing her say his name, her pity…it stirred him more than he could bear. He looked down to see his hands still holding hers, her slender fingers curled into his palms. It felt so natural he hadn't even noticed they were still touching.

I don't want to let go.

He had to let go whether he wanted to or not. So why wouldn't his fingers obey? And why didn't his feet take a step back, away from the temptation zone?

"Is everything okay?"

Matt's voice behind Josh made him jump. He reluctantly let go of Amy's hands and stepped back, even though every bit of him wanted to hold her and comfort her. She'd been very close to his mother before the split and she'd spent lots of holiday time at home in Devon with them.

Their last Christmas together was one of his best memories. Amy had got Dad to wear a paper hat from a cracker and had forced them all to play Pictionary. He could almost see the flickering fire and hear the laughter. Amy had flung her arms around him when she'd seen the antique silver hare brooch he'd saved up to buy her, after she'd admired it in a shop window.

He struggled to compose himself and couldn't look at Matt. He hadn't told the lads about Amy because these things had a habit of spreading. Once they knew, there'd be no keeping it from Juliet. And this week was difficult enough without having to deal with that.

"What's going on?" Matt's tone was hard and unfriendly. "Why is Amy crying? What have you done to upset her?"

Josh sighed heavily. It seemed he had no option. He had to tell him.

"I was just telling her about my parents." He turned to Matt, coolly staring him down. "Amy knew them personally because, well, we used to be a couple."

Matt stared at him and then turned to Amy, as though seeking confirmation.

She nodded. "He's telling the truth, he hasn't done anything to upset me. Well not today anyway."

The muttered barb at the end of her sentence wounded him as it had no doubt been intended to. Had he really hurt her that badly?

I had to do it the way I did. I did it for you Amy…

"Right." Matt's hard gaze flickered between the two of them and rested on Josh. "Can I have a word mate?"

Josh shrugged. "I don't know. Are you okay Amy?"

She looked up at him, startled. "Um, sure."

He didn't believe her. There was a blankness to her expression that made him feel unutterably sad.

I want to make her smile again.

Matt propelled him none too gently down the corridor towards his room and once in, he shut the door firmly behind them.

"What the bloody hell do you think you're doing?" Matt asked.

"What the hell do *you* think you're doing?" Josh tried to bite back the full force of his irritation. It wasn't fair to take out all his frustration on Matt.

"I'm doing my job as your best man." Matt was breathing heavily. Josh had never seen him this angry before, in all the years they'd worked together. "I saw you holding hands and staring into Amy's eyes. The chalet girls don't come as part of the ski holiday package you know."

Huh.

That was a bit rich considering Matt had been quite happy to take things further with Amy himself.

Josh didn't know what to say. How could he say it meant nothing? If he started lying now, where would it all end?

"As I said, we used to be an item, for about three years."

Matt sighed heavily and dropped down on to the bed. "Shit, I've just realised. She was trying to make you jealous when she kissed me."

"I don't know." Josh shook his head. "That doesn't sound like the kind of thing Amy would do. Not the Amy I knew anyway."

But she's changed.

Then he was hit by a terrible thought, what if it had been him who'd changed her?

"She did apologise." Matt leant back on the bed. "Still, it's not great for the old ego, just as well Amelia seems more amenable. But we're going off topic. You know Juliet would go mad if she walked in and found you staring into another girl's eyes, and not without good reason. Hey, don't she and the other girls check into Hotel Paradis today? Have you heard from her?"

"Erm, not sure, I haven't checked." Josh pulled his mobile out of his pocket. "No, but she did say she wouldn't contact me before the wedding. She didn't want me bothering her while she was on her spa break with the girls. Phones were banned, anyway."

"Are you going over to see her?"

"No, she's into this superstitious crap about us not seeing each other before the wedding." Josh put his phone away.

"You're going to have to avoid Amy from now on." Matt said, folding his arms over his chest to indicate he still wasn't happy.

Well, that makes two of us.

"I know what I have to do." Josh frowned.

Of course he knew. Hadn't his father always drummed into him that he must always do "the right thing" especially where girls were concerned? But yet again doing the right thing felt bloody awful. Josh had been here before and a part of him had never stopped regretting the choices he'd been forced to make.

And now he was going to have to hurt Amy all over again.

"Amy, have you got a sec?" Holly had a small stack of boxes in her arms. She seemed distracted, anxious even, which was unusual for her.

"Sure. Is everything okay?" Amy went forward to take some of the boxes from her, glad to have someone else's problems to think about for a change.

"Just a tad stressed." Holly smiled a tight smile. "This is the first wedding I've arranged for someone else and it's proving... stressful. The bride-to-be is being a little difficult. Actually forget I said that, it's really unprofessional of me."

Holly sank into a chair and leant forward, head in hands.

"Is she a bit of a bridezilla then?" Amy knew it was bad of her to be glad, but what the hell, she couldn't help it.

"Mmm." Holly smiled ruefully. "It was so much easier with my own wedding last year, but then I suppose some weddings are easier than others!"

"I'm sure that's the case." Amy reassured her. "What was that favour you wanted?"

"Could you take these boxes over to Hotel Paradis?" Holly asked. "You'd be best taking Tash, too, there are rather a lot of them."

"What's in them?" Amy felt conflicted, wanting on the one hand to escape the chalet, but not wanting to bump into Josh's bridezilla of a fiancée. Maybe she'd be able to dump them in the hotel reception and then leg it before she had the chance to come across her.

"There's a mock-up of the table decorations and samples of the food we'll be serving at the mountain cantine after the chapel ceremony. It is all as I discussed with her by email, so there shouldn't really be any problems. I don't know why she's insisting she sees them at this late stage, but whatever the customer wants…" Holly groaned. "Sorry, do you mind Amy? Only I've got so much left to do I can't really spare the time this evening."

I can do this. It will be fine.

Like immersion therapy. She needed to get over Josh, therefore helping with his wedding to another woman was actually the best thing she could be doing.

Yeah right!

But she had to help Holly, partly because she was her boss, but also because she liked her. She'd never seen Holly looking so stressed and knew she had to do all she could.

"It's fine Holly. Tash and I will have it all covered." Amy tried to smile, but the news about Josh's parents seemed to have shaken the ability to smile out of her. She never would've imagined…

Somehow she pictured them in their period cottage on Exmoor forever; his dad taking their two border terriers out for walks while his mother worked on a new patchwork project.

It'd felt like grieving the first time round she'd lost them, when Josh dumped her, but now she felt the full force of that grief all over again.

"I'll go and get Tash and we'll head off." Amy walked over to the door before Holly could notice anything was up. Usually she had good radar for upset staff, but it'd clearly been knocked off course by bridezilla.

"Thanks Amy," Holly called out after her.

Amy walked into the dorm room. Tash was lying on her back on her bunk, listening to her iPod. Amy waved to catch her attention and Tash removed her headphones.

"You're not going out tonight are you?" Amy asked.

"No, thought I'd have a night in. You okay?"

"I'm fine." Amy shrugged. Maybe if she said it enough times it would come true. "But I need your help. Holly's stressed out. She wants us to take some stuff up to the Hotel Paradis…where the…well, where the bride is staying."

Tash whistled. "Josh's intended you mean? And you agreed?"

"I don't see how I had any choice, but anyway, Holly is stressed so of course I said yes. It's not fair to ask her to get the others to do it, because they did dinner tonight."

Tash swung her legs over the side of the bunk and climbed down. "I bet you're curious. Don't you want to meet the woman who's marrying your ex? Suss out the competition?"

"She's not the competition," Amy said quickly. "I'm not into splitting up relationships. That's even if I wanted Josh back. Which I don't."

She'd been cheated on, post Josh, and it wasn't something she could do to another woman.

Tash laughed and winked. "Honest guv. I believe you. Thousands wouldn't."

Heat crept up Amy's neck. "Shall we get ready to go then? I think we'll have to bother with our ski jackets and scarves, it's freezing out there tonight."

"And pretty hot in here if your face is anything to go by." Tash smirked and pulled a hoodie on over her long-sleeved t-shirt. "Okay, okay, I'll shut up."

"Chance'd be a fine thing," Amy muttered.

"I promise, no more teasing. Not for, ooh, at least ten minutes." Tash linked her arm through Amy's.

"That long, eh?" Amy stuck her tongue out at her as they headed for their coats. "Let's just get this over and done with."

They trudged through the snow, their breath visible in the freezing night air that stung their cheeks and made their noses run – the only parts left exposed to the elements. Christmas trees outside shops were decorated with twinkling white lights or classic red bows. Perhaps they stopped you at the border and confiscated any tacky tinsel or flashing Santas?

Bare branches of trees were also decorated with tiny white lights that reflected on the sparkling surface of the snow. But somehow Amy wasn't feeling very Christmassy.

"So, what's the plan then?" Tash asked.

"We leave these boxes at reception and make a run for it," Amy replied.

"Really?" Tash turned to look at her. "You don't want to see what she looks like?"

"I'm not sure." Amy sighed, kicking at the fresh snowfall not yet cleared from the pavements. "Part of me wants to. Maybe I should get it over with? Perhaps it would help me…you know, accept it?"

I need to find a way to say goodbye forever. I have to let go.

"Closure?" Tash asked.

"Hmm," Amy mumbled.

Funny how the impending wedding felt more like a funeral. In a way it was a funeral for her – a death of all the hopes she'd secretly been hanging on to. But she had to accept she'd been wrong with her conviction that she and Josh were meant to be together, that somehow he'd come back to her. Did her believing that mean she really did forgive him, deep down?"

She aimed another kick at a fresh snowdrift and almost lost her footing.

"Hey, careful there! Was that Josh's head you were imagining by any chance?" Tash asked.

"No, I was just thinking about all those films where they go on about 'the one' and how 'it's meant to be.' I blame them. It's all a load of crap, basically, isn't it?" Amy smiled grimly.

"You're still really into him aren't you?" Tash asked quietly.

"Yes." The truth escaped her lips before Amy could shoot back the bolt to keep it in.

"Can you forgive him for whatever he did to hurt you so much?" Tash stopped walking and had turned to face Amy. "I know you didn't tell us everything. You didn't need to. We've all been there in one way or the other."

Who had hurt Tash? It didn't seem the right time to ask.

"I've been asking the same question and the thing is, I don't know," Amy answered honestly. "He wasn't there for me when I really needed him. I can't help thinking if he'd been there then things might've been different."

Amy felt tears pressing at her eyelids and blinked them back fiercely.

I am not going to be depressed again. I'm simply not. Don't I know better by now than to waste time on the 'if onlys?'

"Unless he hit you, cheated on you, stole from you or turned out to be married to someone else I'd say it's worth trying to forgive him." Tash rested her boxes on an icy railing, her face sombre. "It's up to you of course, but I bet you'd feel better if you did."

Amy looked hard at Tash. "God, what type of men have you been out with Tash? No, don't answer that. What about revenge? I thought you believed in it."

"Of course." Tash grinned, her serious expression vanishing as she carried on walking towards the centre of Verbier. "You punish him first and *then* you forgive him, obviously."

"Oh, right." Amy trudged on through the fresh snow, her feet dragging as the Hotel Paradis came closer into view. Her heart rate increased to a persistent thrumming against her ribcage. If only she could have Tash's no-nonsense approach to life. She always seemed to have an answer for everything.

"Ready?" Tash raised an eyebrow as they approached the revolving doors.

Amy nodded and they made their way to reception. She kept a look out for anyone who could possibly be Juliet.

"Hi there, Niall," Tash flashed a smile at the night duty receptionist. Amy recognised the Irish guy by the fair complexion and freckles that gave away that he wasn't a native. She'd seen him out and about in town. There were so many different nationalities in this town it was often easier to try English first, before her rusty school French. "We've got these boxes for a Miss…what's her name Amy?"

"Juliet Davidson." Amy put her boxes onto the reception counter. "Can we just leave them here and go?"

Niall pulled a face. "No, I'm afraid not. She gave specific instructions they were to be brought straight up to her room. It's room number three one two. I'd help you with the boxes only I can't leave the desk."

"Oh." Amy hesitated. If she'd thought her heart was beating rapidly when she entered the hotel, now her pulse raced so fast she felt faint.

"We'll go straight up. Thanks Niall. Maybe we'll catch you later for a drink?" Tash made her way to the lifts and Amy reluctantly followed her.

"Not tonight, I'm on duty until six a.m." Niall winked at Amy and lowered his voice. "Maybe another night. Good luck with the bride-to-be. I'll be here if you need to sound off afterwards."

Great, yet more confirmation that Juliet was difficult. What on earth was Josh doing marrying someone like that? Maybe it was the wedding stress making her "difficult". Weddings did turn some quite ordinary woman into bridezillas.

After all, her own sister had turned into a complete nightmare. No one had so much as exhaled in the family home until Emily had set off on her honeymoon.

She trudged towards the lift.

"Hurry up Amy." Tash awkwardly balanced the boxes while pressing the door hold button.

Amy reluctantly hurried towards the lift and stepped in. Once the doors had closed she checked her reflection in the mirror and hastily took off her faux-fur hat, then ran her fingers through her hair in a futile attempt to neaten it up.

She turned to Tash. "The last thing I need right now is hat-hair."

"Here." Tash put the boxes on the floor and reached into her bag, handing her a lipstick. "Put this on while you're at it."

Amy took it, not wanting to say she never usually wore lipstick, only lip gloss or a slick of Vaseline. She put it on anyway and had to admit the bright-red shade looked good, defining her lips. Somehow it gave her more confidence. Lipstick girl wouldn't take any crap from bridezilla.

"I don't think there's any way she'll know who I am, do you?" Amy said, suddenly nervous.

"Maybe not, but you need to be prepared for her finding out." Tash shrugged. "We've got the advantage on her – the element of surprise is very important in psychological warfare."

"Warfare?" Amy laughed. "Surely it's not as bad as all that?"

The doors opened onto the third floor and she stepped out, her heart beating hard in her chest.

"Of course it is," Tash said. "What would you do without me? Even if you don't want Josh back this is still a competition."

"Hmm, I suppose." Amy took a deep breath in to relax her body. "You're right about one thing – I am lucky to have you."

"No problem." Tash walked briskly towards room three one two. "I've been there myself. I know how much it can help to have the right friends around."

Before Amy could ask her about it Tash had knocked on the door.

"Come in!" A posh voice ordered imperiously from inside the room.

Tash raised her eyebrows and knocked again. After all, they

didn't have a key card to let themselves in, and their arms were full of boxes.

"Oh, for God's sake!" A woman Amy presumed to be Juliet swung the door open.

Whatever Amy had been expecting, it hadn't been this. She might as well be looking in a mirror – Juliet was petite like her, with fair skin and hair and green, cat-like eyes.

She looks like me.

Albeit a better groomed, more polished and older version of herself. How Amy might look if she had the time and money to lavish on her appearance. Amy's head buzzed.

Josh picked someone who looked like me!

The thoughts consumed her so much she actually forgot to speak.

"Well?" Juliet snapped. "Can't you talk or something?"

It was tempting to pretend she was in fact mute, just to wrong-foot Juliet. But it would be a hard pretence to keep up long-term.

"Hi there," Tash said, not remotely bothered by Juliet's irritable glare. "We've come from Chalet Repos. Holly sent us with some things you wanted."

"Well obviously." Juliet scowled. "I'd have thought you'd have the brains to ask reception for a key card. Well I suppose you're here now. Bring them in then."

Amy walked into the room and smiled awkwardly at the group of women sitting on the sofa and chairs. She put her boxes on the dressing table and floor and shot a desperate look at Tash.

"Let's go." Amy mouthed.

They headed back to the door but Juliet barred their way. "And where the hell do you think you're going?"

"Sorry?" Amy met Juliet's eye, startled and irritated she'd automatically apologised. She wished she hadn't, now. All she could think about was Josh making love to Juliet and she couldn't erase those images from her mind.

Juliet tutted. "Well obviously I need you to serve the food and take notes so you can report back to Holly whatever her name is. Where is your notebook?"

Amy felt almost compelled to look in her pockets, even though she knew for a fact she didn't have a notebook anywhere.

"I'll take notes on my phone." Tash pulled a smartphone out of her pocket. "We'll take the boxes out on the balcony to get them organised and bring things in then. We weren't expecting to do more than deliver them, so we'll need a minute to prepare."

"Honestly" Juliet huffed. "Josh convinced me to give this ski-themed wedding a try and I thought 'why not'? It sounded different but I'm not convinced that girl knows what she's doing."

"The wedding last year went without a hitch." Tash replied, a hint of steel in her voice.

Amy felt too angry to trust herself to speak. They moved out onto the freezing balcony, but they hadn't even closed the doors before they heard one of Juliet's friends comment. "She obviously can't get the staff."

Amy realised she was grinding her teeth and had to resist the urge to slam the doors shut behind them.

"What a bitch." Tash rolled her eyes dramatically.

"Shh, she'll hear us," Amy hissed.

"And your point is?" Tash grinned.

"And I can't believe you didn't tell her to piss off."

"I told you, this is warfare, we're gathering information, getting to know our enemy." Tash said. "And she's a bitch. Don't tell me you missed that?"

"She could be stressed out by the wedding. Lots of brides become a bit…stressy." Amy knelt down and began to open up the boxes to work out what was in them. She tried to locate the food samples first.

Tash leant against the balcony railing, seemingly unbothered. "Don't make excuses for her, a bitch is a bitch. Trust me, my bitch radar never fails."

"But Josh wouldn't marry a bitch, he's lov…too nice." Amy's

cheeks burned with heat despite the cold night air.

I nearly said he was lovely. Get over it Amy. He's marrying her and that's that.

"She's not a woman's woman. I bet she behaves quite differently around men. I'd put money on Josh knowing a different Juliet." Tash moved unhurriedly to the boxes and took the film-covered platters of mini-rostis and raclette, while Amy picked up the plate with the very tempting Swiss chocolates.

How can Josh be marrying that woman? How?

"I don't know why we're serving these to her. It's a bit late to change her mind." Amy felt her heart sink down to her boots as they headed back into the room. "Holly will go ballistic if any drastic changes are made at this stage."

When they entered the room Juliet kept her back to them and continued her conversation with her friends, even though she must've felt the draught of icy air from the open doors. Then she waved a hand at them impatiently, signalling they should bring the platters over, but still didn't turn to look at them.

Amy knew Juliet had no idea who she was. She was like the snooty guests they get at Chalet Repos occasionally, the ones to whom all staff were invisible.

"Oh, you are awful." A brunette with a Cleopatra bob shrieked with laughter. "I still can't believe you hooked up with Tom in Ibiza. Still I suppose it was worth having a final farewell shag."

"Who says it was a farewell shag?" Juliet raised her eyebrows as she took a mini rosti from the tray Tash carried and eyed it dubiously.

Amy struggled not to drop the tray.

Did I really hear that right?

What kind of woman went around boasting in front of strangers? Oh, except she and Tash didn't count because they were staff, practically sub-human.

"Are you sure you're ready to get married?" A blonde looked disdainfully at the tray. "I know Josh is a honey and everything but if you like the thrill of the chase… look I don't do carbs or dairy okay?"

Her last remark had been irritably addressed to Tash.

"You'll go hungry in Switzerland then," Tash muttered and Juliet turned to look at her, annoyed.

"Where is the fondue? There is supposed to be a savoury and a chocolate fondue for each table," Juliet snapped.

"We could hardly bring a fondue, we'd need gas for a start." Amy found her voice, her irritation rushing to the surface.

Juliet pursed her mouth, cross lines appearing on her forehead. "Bring the table decorations, then, we don't have all evening."

Then she turned her back on them again.

Amy bit her lip as she strode over to the balcony windows with Tash, fury bubbling up in her. They left the doors open this time, not caring if the occupants of the room got cold.

Juliet's voice carried out to the balcony.

"The thrill of an affair is just as good, trust me." Juliet laughed. "Anyway, it's always been my plan to marry before I'm thirty. Josh is a fantastic catch. He'll treat me well and look after me financially. He's inherited this huge period cottage in the Exmoor National Park. Once he sells that we'll be rolling in it."

Amy's hands shook and she dropped the lid of one of the boxes. Her grief at the news of Josh's parents' accident was still so fresh that Juliet's words made her feel like she'd been slapped in the face.

How can she, how can she be so callous, so grasping?… so…

"And Josh wants to settle down too and start a family as soon as possible. I'm fine with that. Everyone cheats nowadays, just look at the statistics. It's really no big deal."

"But Josh is really fit, why would you even need anyone else?" One of the girls sitting on the sofa asked.

"Variety is the spice of life girls," Juliet grinned. "But it doesn't pay the bills."

Amy's hands closed into fists.

"It's not worth it," Tash whispered. "It's not worth losing your job over."

"I thought you always spoke your mind," Amy hissed back fiercely, accusingly.

"I know where to draw the line and what I can get away with. I pick my battles." Tash gestured behind them into the room. "That is one warzone you don't want to go charging into, this is only a recce, remember?"

"I suppose," Amy whispered. She stared at the contents of the box Tash had just opened; table decorations with red and white roses and Swiss-style decorations for the reception at the mountain cantine.

These are for Josh's wedding…to her!

Her temples pounded and spots swam in front of her eyes. She tried to breathe slowly.

"You go down to reception. I'll say you've been taken ill," Tash muttered, looking over to Juliet, who was still deep in conversation with her friends. "Okay?"

"Thanks." Amy nodded gratefully.

"Just go, she probably won't notice, if she does, just keep going. You could always pretend you need a bathroom. Go." Tash took Amy's elbow and gave her a little push.

Amy walked swiftly towards the door, trying to keep down the bile as she passed Juliet. There was no need to pretend, she really did need a bathroom.

She was going to be sick.

CHAPTER FIVE

Amy walked back to Chalet Repos, her heart pounding. It felt like she was sleep walking. Her ski season working holiday had turned into a nightmare.

I have to talk to Josh.

She found him in the living room, stoking the fire with a poker, prodding viciously at the logs and staring into the flames. Matt and the other guys weren't there, thank God. Why was Josh alone on what was supposed to be his stag party and why did he look so grim?

Whatever the reason, here they were. Just the two of them. It had to be a sign she was meant to do this.

Her hands shook a little as she approached, so she hastily clasped them together in front of her before Josh could notice. Should she sit? Stand? For a moment she said nothing, simply stood, staring at him, trying to summon the courage to do this.

I've got no choice. I have to tell him.

"Josh," she spoke his name quietly, reluctant to break the silence of the room.

He jerked backwards, turning his head towards her, startled.

"Amy." He got to his feet and the obvious pleasure in his dark-brown eyes was replaced by a flash of anxiety. He scanned the room and then heaved out a sigh upon finding it empty apart from them.

"I need to talk to you, but it's, um, personal. I think we should go to your room. If we stay here anyone could walk in." Amy glanced towards the corridor leading to the guest rooms.

"I'm not sure that's a good idea." Josh frowned.

"Why? I only want to talk. I'm not going to throw myself at you." She folded her arms across her chest, her anger rising. Just what did he think she was going to do? She felt insulted.

"Right," Josh said, staring at her, his eyes reflecting his concern and…something else she couldn't quite fathom. "Okay then."

He gestured for Amy to go first. She was sure she could feel his eyes assessing her, skimming over her body as she walked. Anticipation flickered deep inside her.

Concentrate Amy. You're not here for that; you're on a mission.

Once in his room she hesitated. Should she sit on the bed? That probably wasn't a good idea.

She turned to face him, wishing she could close the gap between them and feel his arms around her, comforting her. Her fingers itched to reach out and touch him again, so she clasped them together to prevent any involuntary movement. It had been such an odd evening already, she felt like anything might be possible. She certainly couldn't trust her body.

Josh stared, wordlessly, a slight frown on his handsome face but their old connection was definitely there. She felt the full force of it now and she allowed herself to drink it in. Now she remembered why she'd been avoiding his gaze ever since he'd got here.

One look had been all it'd taken back then, when she met him for the first time. One look and she'd been smitten by his sexy grin and eyes that lit up every time he laughed.

"So?" Josh seemed to be having difficulty speaking. His stare left her feeling unnerved.

Was he angry with her? Well sod him, she was doing this for him after all.

This wasn't about revenge and it wasn't because she wanted him back. This was because she, well…cared about him. His happiness mattered to her.

"I've met Juliet," she said bluntly, watching him closely, wanting to understand what he felt for Juliet and why on earth he felt it.

Perhaps she's lovely really and it's the wedding that's turned her into a cow.

"Oh?" His eyes widened. So, she'd managed to startle him twice in one evening.

"You can't marry her. Really, you just can't." The words streamed out of her mouth and she couldn't stop them. She hadn't meant to do it like this.

"Amy, I know this must be upsetting for you…" Josh laid a hand on her arm and a warmth spread slowly through her body.

Heat crept up her neck and across her face as she burned with mortification.

"No, you don't understand." She shook her head crossly. "I'm not doing a 'don't marry her, marry me' speech. You're getting it all wrong."

"So?" Josh withdrew his hand from her arm with what appeared to be reluctance. Or was that just wishful thinking on her part?

"I overheard her talking to her friends and there's something you need to know." She fidgeted awkwardly on the spot. It had seemed so urgent that she tell him, she hadn't spent enough time thinking about how she should do it.

"Go on then." Josh's mouth was set in a grim line as he folded his arms across his broad chest to listen to her.

"She's having an affair and plans to carry on, you know, doing it after you get married." She searched his eyes for some recognition he believed her, that she was getting through to him, but the shutters were well and truly down. She had no idea what he was thinking.

"Amy, I know you're upset with me for some reason." Josh sighed.

For some reason? For some reason?

Momentarily speechless she stared at him, suddenly feeling like she was staring at a stranger.

"And you clearly want to piss me off," Josh's frown deepened even further. "All that stuff with Matt the other night? That was meant to annoy me, wasn't it?"

Amy's face flushed even hotter. "I'm telling you the truth Josh, don't you know me well enough to know I wouldn't lie about something like this?"

"I thought I knew you." Josh leant back against the wall, breathing out with a deep sigh. "But kissing Matt to try and score points against me, well…I don't know if I do know you any more."

That stung. How could she explain it hadn't only been about getting back at him but needing to feel attractive and desired in the face of his rejection? But if she didn't tell the truth now she'd destroy any credibility she had left with him.

"Okay, I was a little angry," she admitted. "Matt's nice and he seemed okay with it." She sank down onto the edge of the bed, her trembling legs refusing to hold her up any longer, adrenalin leaving her in a whoosh. "If you want the whole truth, I'm not gluten-intolerant either, I made that up."

Great, why had that slipped out as well?

"Why on earth would you make that up?" Josh shook his head, bewildered.

"There was a bit of extra chilli in your tartlet, well, more than a bit really. Then I decided it was childish and I couldn't go through with it."

"So that's why you switched plates and were acting so weirdly?" Josh heaved another sigh and came to sit next to her on the edge of the bed, just far enough away so they weren't touching. He looked…gutted. "Do you really hate me that much?"

There was raw pain in his voice. It broke her heart and she had to squeeze her eyes tight shut to stop the tears from falling. Silently she shook her head.

I can't tell him now. Not here and like this…

"And telling me all this is supposed to make me believe you're telling the truth about Juliet?" he turned to examine her and the expression in his eyes made her want to climb onto his lap and tell him everything, to make him like and respect her again.

"I am telling the truth, Josh," she replied sadly. "Coming to talk to you wasn't about us or even about me. I'm telling you because I want you to be happy. She doesn't deserve you and I'm having a hard job believing you love her. Why are you marrying her?"

Josh stared at Amy, trying to work her out. A thousand questions swirling around his mind in a blizzard of words. Did she have an agenda? What was she hoping to accomplish? *Is she telling me the truth?*

But the biggest question of all was the one she had just asked him. Why was he marrying Juliet? Because she'd come along at the right time. Because he'd given up hope of getting back in contact with Amy, convinced she was happy and had moved on with someone else.

The day he'd got the call telling him about Mum and Dad had changed everything for him. He'd taken their support for granted, they'd provided a home, a network, somewhere he knew he could always go back to. Home. He was tired of travelling the world alone and living as an ex-pat bachelor. He needed roots, ties… a family of his own.

He'd wanted to get married and so had Juliet so…

Did he love her like he'd loved Amy back at uni? No, but then that kind of first love was unique, you couldn't expect to…

Oh God.

He looked at Amy, at the pain in her eyes. All this time he'd been trying to do the right thing and yet he'd hurt her. Hurt her so much she'd wanted revenge.

It would be the ultimate revenge for her to ruin your wedding…

But Amy was right; he just couldn't believe she'd be capable of lying about something like this. And his body burned for her every bit as much as it had the first time round. Even more this time because he knew what it was like to make love to her. He knew what he was missing.

"What are you thinking?"

"I'm thinking I'm getting married soon and this is a gigantic mess."

"You're still getting married?" Her eyes widened in shock.

I have to do the right thing, whatever that is…

"I can't call off the wedding and jilt Juliet on the say-so of an ex-girlfriend. That would hardly be fair to her." He gripped the edge of the mattress with his hands, needing to stop them from reaching out to Amy. She shouldn't be here in his room, it was too close, too tempting and he was so not the guy who cheated on his fiancée, whatever might or might not have been going on.

Two wrongs didn't make a right.

Amy's telling the truth and you know it, deep down in your gut.

But he couldn't make decisions with his gut. Hadn't he been trained to use his brain, to apply logic to all problems and reason them out? Logic said he had no evidence and Amy had, of her own admission, wanted to get revenge.

As for his heart, his gut…that was weakness, his own desires. What would his father have said if he broke the heart of his fiancée and called off the wedding purely because his desires were leading him in another direction?

Pandering to desire was weak and he had to be strong. To act in a way they would've been proud of.

"So my word isn't enough; you don't believe me?" Amy got shakily to her feet, anger flashing in her eyes. "And if I told you Tash can confirm it?"

"The girl with pink streaks in her hair?" Josh asked.

"Yes," Amy replied defiantly. "I suppose you'll say I put her up to it."

"I wouldn't say anything," Josh felt exasperated. "But she did help you with the chilli, didn't she? You said 'we' earlier. You've got to see I can't act without evidence."

Amy walked to the door, her hand on the knob, then turned and stared. He felt it, their old connection. Of course he did. The connection he'd assumed was simply what you always felt with your girlfriend, that he'd presumed he'd find again once he got over having to let Amy go.

But he never had felt it with anyone again.

Amy had half opened the door to leave when she hesitated and turned again, her head held high and eyes suspiciously bright. "Just one thing, Josh. Why did you break up with me?"

He met her stare.

"I thought I was doing the right thing," he said. "We were too young to settle down. If you'd come to Saudi with me we would've had to marry because of the laws there. And abandon your teacher training and been stuck on an ex-pat compound. Could you really have been happy sitting around doing nothing? You were so passionate about your teaching course, I couldn't force you to give up your dreams. It would've been selfish."

Her face didn't alter, but her knuckles on the hand grasping the doorknob had turned white.

"I couldn't turn the job down, Amy," Josh softened his voice, desperately wanting her to understand, really understand. "There weren't tons of jobs to go round then, you know that. For every good position there were twenty or thirty of us engineering graduates pursuing it. I had a student loan to pay off and I wanted to pay my parents back too, so they could go on the cruise they'd been talking about taking one day…"

He gripped the edge of the bed, fighting the surge of emotion.

"I see." Amy's eyes were downcast now, her head turned slightly away from him.

"It doesn't mean I didn't regret…" The words choked in his throat and he couldn't say any more. It wasn't wise to say more. The tension in the air was palpable, emotional vibrations rocking them both. Even though there was a physical gap between them he felt closer to Amy than he had to anyone in years.

He knew she understood.

Finally Amy looked up, her face anguished. "Josh, I can't let you marry her, I can't. I'll get you your proof."

Amy stared out of the window at the dark, threatening sky. Chalet Repos was practically submerged in thick, grey snow cloud; she could barely see down to the next chalet, never mind the valley below. Thick, white flakes of snow fell steadily, silently to the ground, blanketing Verbier in yet more white gold.

She stood with her back to the table where Josh's group and the girls finished their breakfast. Scott and Holly had appeared to join them for coffee. Her own appetite was conspicuous by its absence. She didn't know how to be near Josh in other company; it felt like a constant battle not to meet his eye or give herself away. As far as she knew, only Matt and the girls knew she and Josh had history.

The knowledge she had to do something to stop the wedding felt like solidifying concrete in her stomach. She hugged her arms around her body, still staring at the steadily falling flakes of snow. It was all very well knowing she had to do it but at the moment she hadn't the faintest idea how she could achieve it.

"Hi there, how's the groom this morning?" Holly's question made Amy turn round despite herself.

"Great thanks." Josh replied politely enough, but when Amy glanced at his face she saw the familiar twitch at the corner of his mouth that told her he was lying through his teeth.

She perched on the back of a leather armchair, trying to appear disinterested.

Scott looked up from his iPad. "Bad news, I'm afraid guys, I just looked up the weather forecast and there's a big storm forecast, I think they'll be closing the lifts today. You might get a run in if you're quick, but I really wouldn't recommend it."

"That's a shame," Matt replied. "What do you think, Josh? It's your call."

"I don't think we should risk it." Josh frowned and then looked over at Paul and Mark. "Are you two okay with that?"

They both grunted, shrugging as they continued to pile croissants and pain au chocolat onto their plates.

"You could go down to the Christmas markets at Montreux," Holly suggested, sipping at her coffee.

"Ooh, I've been wanting to go down to the Montreux market again," Amelia said. "It was such fun last year. I definitely recommend it. I think I got all my Christmas presents in one trip and the food was amazing. They do these lovely hot waffles and chocolate pancakes."

"Why don't you come with us?" Matt said, smiling warmly at Amelia. Then, as though an afterthought, hastily turned to look round at the rest of the group. "All of you, I mean."

"Could do," Scott said thoughtfully, scratching his stubble. "I need to see a man about a reindeer."

"Seriously?" Sophie giggled.

"Yes, to pull the sleigh from the chapel to the reception." Holly glanced warily at Josh and plastered a professional smile on her face. "Last-minute change, we're having reindeer pulling the sleigh instead of horses. No problem, though, we've got it sorted I think."

"Reindeer?" Josh's frown deepened even further. "I thought we were skiing to…"

"Direct request from the bride, she said you'd both agreed…" Holly chewed at her bottom lip, anxiety shining in her eyes.

"It's fine, I probably just forgot to read an email or something." Josh shrugged and did his best to put a polite smile on his face.

Amy had to fold her arms tightly across her chest to prevent herself from reaching out to him. Just like Josh to smile politely instead of saying "What the fuck?" like a normal person.

"Luckily I've got a contact at Chateau Chillon," Scott said, reaching across the table for a croissant. "Well, they always have reindeer and I can borrow them for a few hours, for a price of course."

The storm clouds outside had nothing on the flash of irritation in Josh's eyes, although he clearly did his best to hide it. How could Amy spend the day in his company and not mouth off about the horrendous mistake he was making? Mouth off *again* that was. Josh already knew her views. In the words of Elvis what was needed now was a little less conversation and a little more action.

"I'm not sure I've got time to come." Holly rubbed a hand over her eyes.

"And I'm on evening meal duty with Tash so one us should stay behind really, I don't mind volunteering," Amy gabbled quickly, keen to get her point across. She hovered at the back of the group, waiting for her chance to escape.

I so do not have time for this, I've got a wedding to cancel.

She glanced guiltily at Holly, who was probably thinking the same, only substituting the word "cancel" for the word "arrange". Amy liked Holly and yet she was working to undermine all her hard work. There would be consequences.

"We're all going," Scott announced firmly. "We can get something to eat down at the markets. They do all kinds of food, not just snacks."

Amy sighed, knowing she was beaten. Scott might be easy-going in some respects, but he wasn't someone you disobeyed.

"Well, if we are going I just need to send a few emails first." Holly stared levelly at her husband. "Thirty minutes to get ready and we'll meet at the minibus. Don't forget, you'll need your warmest clothes. We might be going down to the valley floor, but it gets really cold, trust me."

"But what about the storm?" Amy hissed at Tash as they left the dorm room.

"The markets are down in Montreux; the storm might not even reach it down to the lake, you know what mountain weather is like." Tash shrugged. "Who cares? We've got the day off and don't have to cook tonight, that's all that matters."

Amy stared down at her feet, cheeks burning. She couldn't share her plan to stop the wedding with Tash, or anyone for that matter;

they'd only try to talk her out of it. Not that she had much of a plan yet. She just had to use the time to think.

"Is it Josh?" Tash asked.

"Ssh." Amy grabbed Tash's arm, glancing anxiously behind them, hoping no one had heard. "Not now, please Tash. This really is hard enough already without the whole world knowing about it."

Tash raised an impressive eyebrow at her, scarlet eye shadow accentuating her cat-like eyes and making them seem even bluer than usual.

Amy knew what that eyebrow meant.

"Later".

Tash wasn't about to let her off the hook for too long. Amy's mouth tightened. She was going to stop the wedding, with or without her blessing.

Amy reached into her bag for her purse. Retail therapy was not her first choice of distraction for dealing with stress, but if the ski lifts were going to be closed…

"Amy, can I have a word?" Amelia touched Amy's arm, making her jump.

"Sure." Amy eyed Amelia warily.

Not another intervention? But that was more Tash's style than Amelia's.

"Is there anything between you and Matt?" Amelia asked, her cheeks flushed unnaturally pink. "Only I saw you two kissing the other night and um…we've been getting on really well."

Amy breathed out in relief. So that was it. It was a little galling that Matt could transfer his affections so rapidly. But she was pleased. Matt was a nice guy and who knew? He might smooth off some of Amelia's sharper corners.

"No, not at all." Amy smiled. "He's all yours Amelia. Go for it."

"Er, thanks." Amelia's features softened into a smile as she sat down on the lower bunk and took out her make-up bag.

How easy it would be if I could fall for someone unattached and let Josh go.

For a moment Amy wavered. But this wasn't about her, it was about protecting Josh.

Or was it? Really? Amy stared at her reflection in her own compact mirror. A pale face stared back at her, a sleepless night evident in her bloodshot eyes. Was she lying to herself?

Just a little bit, maybe. She wanted to protect Josh, but she also wanted…more. Amy pushed down a surge of emotion.

Not now, I can't deal with thinking about the future now.

The lake shore at Montreux was crowded, the path lined with lit wooden chalet stalls. The Alps on the other side of the lake were swathed in thick, angry cloud, but above Montreux the sky was clear, the air biting and crisp.

Amy pulled her scarf around her neck, tucking it into her coat to keep out the cold air, her eyes drawn to the exquisitely made Christmas decorations, the nutcracker soldiers and gingerbread houses. She'd already bought some quirky felt purses from a stall in the Mongolian Yurt. They'd do as presents for the girls and Holly. The handmade soaps and scrumptious-looking Swiss chocolates looked great too; her mum would love them, not that she'd get them home in time for Christmas.

She'd enjoyed seeing the re-enacted medieval market at Chateau Chillon while Scott had gone off in search of his reindeer contact, but her French hadn't been up to understanding the commentaries and story-telling.

Reindeers? For frick's sake!

Poor Scott and Holly being bombarded with all these last-minute demands. What next? Would Juliet insist Father Christmas drove the sleigh?

This market at Montreux was more her thing – shiny, sparkly, pretty things. Delicate strings of flower-lights caught her attention. She wanted to buy a couple of sets, but where would she put them? Maybe it was time to look for a job where she could rent her own place, however tiny.

They all wandered into the large, covered food court next to the Ferris wheel, passing trees decorated with tiny white lights, sparkling against bare branches. Carols filled the air, piped through the sound system, some in French, some in English. The air was full of delicious smells, savoury and sweet, of roasting meat and frying pancakes. As she stared at the variety of food on offer, from waffles to tartiflette and fondue, Amy's stomach gave an involuntary rumble, bemoaning the absence of breakfast.

"Hungry?" Josh stood close behind her, leaning in so he could be heard over the music. She felt a shiver of desire tickling her spine at his close proximity.

"Is my stomach rumbling so loudly you can hear it over the sound of the carols?" Amy smiled awkwardly, turning her head to face him, close enough to feel the warmth of his body.

Step away Amy. Expose Juliet first and stop Josh making a hideous mistake. Maybe, then we'll see…

"Hey, I know you, remember? You were always hungry. And I noticed you didn't eat much at breakfast," Josh replied, inching closer, his face so near that she could lose herself in his eyes, feel herself melting as the noise and crowds around her dissolved into nothingness. Her mind airbrushed everything out, leaving just her and Josh.

Her chest ached with suppressed emotion.

Kiss me.

"Hey you two, we're all going to the Lumberjack Village." Sophie tugged on the sleeve of Amy's coat, shooting her a meaningful look. "Let's go."

"The Lumberjack Village?" Josh asked

"They have log cabins with open fires in the middle so we can warm up." Sophie linked her arm through Amy's, giving her little choice but to go with her. "Most importantly they have wood-fired pizzas and hot wine!"

"Sounds great." Josh smiled stiffly and walked with them. This time he kept his distance, his eyes dark and expression troubled.

He wants me as much as I want him.

Amy felt dizzy, her vision blurry with sparkling lights. Her senses were overwhelmed by the smells and music and crowds. And most of all by Josh…

I need something to eat, that's all.

She was getting good at this lying to herself lark.

Inside the log cabin Paul and Mark had already grabbed some beers and flanked Tash on either side, warming themselves at the railing around the central fire.

Amy instinctively moved forward towards the heat; despite her warm clothing the tip of her nose had gone cold. The flames flickered and licked around the logs. She watched, mesmerised.

This was how she felt, consumed, alive with the certainty she couldn't just carry on drifting. She couldn't sit back and let Josh walk away. Again. She'd lost Josh once to a job, she wasn't going to lose him to Juliet. The job had been something positive, something good for him, but Juliet, well the word toxic didn't feel too extreme.

Josh had moved to stand next to Holly. She'd engaged him in conversation. Probably about the wedding arrangements.

Amy suddenly felt sick, unable to face the pizza. She looked for the nearest exit and slipped out of the cabin, moving instinctively towards the lake shore, feeling the peaceful draw of the inky-black water lapping against the rocks.

The sun had now dipped down below the line of cloud shrouding the French Alps on the opposite side of the lake from Montreux, turning the sky an awesome amber colour, tingeing the clouds with pink.

It was breathtaking.

Amy forced herself to take some deep breaths as she stumbled towards an elegant wrought-iron bench. She slumped gratefully down onto it. Then her gaze fell on a couple kissing, silhouetted against the setting sun.

It took a minute for Amy to realise it was Amelia and Matt.

She smiled, the first genuine smile to grace her lips in a long while. But then the inevitable sadness swept in. It was so uncomplicated for Matt and Amelia – a snog, a fling and then a possible hook-up back in the UK… Amelia didn't have a wedding to sabotage.

A shiver of fear and cold ran through her. How was she going to stop the wedding? She still didn't have a plan. What she needed was to give Josh an honourable "out". And if she had to obtain that in a dishonourable way, well, so be it.

But if he really wants to marry Juliet, he'll marry her.

A warm, salty tear trickled down her cold cheek. Despite her scarf and gloves her fingers felt numb and she could barely feel her toes in her Ugg boots. Yet she couldn't bring herself to care enough to move back to the fire or move about. The black cloud of depression seemed closer now, no longer on her distant horizon, but hovering, waiting to blot out all the light in her world.

"Amy?" Tash slipped onto the bench beside her. "Come here, sweetheart."

Amy leant towards her and Tash put her arms around her, the warmth and kindness broke through the barrier of restraint and Amy sobbed as she rested her head on Tash's shoulder.

After a few minutes Amy lifted her head and fumbled in her coat pockets for a tissue, eventually locating one.

"Sorry." She blew her nose.

"You have to let him go." Tash said.

"Maybe, maybe not. I've got a plan," Amy replied.

And then, as the sun slid down behind the mountains, she sat with Tash beneath the darkening sky and told her what she was intending to do.

CHAPTER SIX

Amy knew she had to do everything she could to stop Juliet getting her hands on Josh and Josh's money. If his parents weren't around to look out for him, she would have to do the job.

His explanation had swept away the remaining lingering anger she'd directed towards Josh. But wasn't she really just furious at life? She'd turned it all on Josh because that was easier, less scary than admitting life could be capricious and unfair. That people you loved could be suddenly whisked away from you by death or by simply choosing to walk away…

But if anyone could understand that it would be Josh. Having lost his parents like that…well, if she explained about her depression she had a feeling he, of all people, would understand.

Life was difficult enough without toxic people and Amy was sure Juliet was toxic.

Josh was too damn decent, that was the problem.

It was just as well Amy wasn't above a bit of scheming herself, then.

And luckily for Amy, Juliet was arrogant. She'd treated Tash and Amy like invisible nobodies. Probably how she treated all staff; merely a part of the background.

She'd thought she might have to stake out the mountain cantine today to spy on Juliet. After all, everyone stopped at the cantine at some point during the day for lunch or a drink when they wanted a break from the pistes. But an inspired phone call to Niall had got her the information she needed.

"You're not really going through with it, are you?" Sophie asked, her expression disapproving. "Why don't you change your mind and come skiing with us today?"

"I have to do this," Amy said crossly, sorting out a bag to put her swimming stuff in. "I'm getting a day pass for the Hotel Paradis Spa. Apparently Juliet prefers to pamper herself rather than go skiing."

And actively doing something about this is the only way I know how to avoid sliding into depression again.

"I think you should just leave it," Tash said, sliding into her salopettes as she lay on the bunk bed. There wasn't enough space in the small room for all four of them to change at the same time.

"Yeah, if they want to get married, that's their call. There's not much you can do about it." Amelia touched up her make-up using a powder compact. "I think you need to give it up."

"While I appreciate all your advice, I know this is something I need to do," Amy said crossly, throwing her hairbrush, purse, phone and deodorant into the bag.

Look where your previous suggestions got me, girls, and then tell me I need to follow your advice.

She bit back the retort. They'd only been trying to help. If she hadn't been so poleaxed by seeing Josh again maybe she would've been strong enough to reject their advice and suggestions that simply weren't "her".

She'd been drifting along in a daydream for too long, allowing herself to be buffeted and blown wherever the wind took her – from job to job, relationship to relationship, not caring for or committing to anything.

Now, however, she was wide awake; the world around her felt sharper and clearer, as though Josh had adjusted her view finder, bringing her life back into focus.

"Well if you have to do it…" Tash eyed her doubtfully. "Just watch your back, okay. And give me a ring if you need me."

"Thanks, Tash." Amy gave a slightly wobbly smile as she picked up her bag. Then she remembered the waterproof case for her iPhone and threw it into the bag. If she was going to get evidence she couldn't risk her phone getting wet. "I'll see you all later. Have fun."

In the corridor Amy bumped into Holly and Scott.

"Not skiing today?" Scott glanced down at her jeans and tunic dress.

"No, I fancied a swim. Thought I'd get a day pass at the Hotel Paradis Spa." Amy felt the heat creeping up her neck, her body always gave her away when she was stressed.

"Sounds nice. "Holly smiled wistfully. "Wish I could come too but there's too much wedding prep to do. God forbid I get any tiny detail wrong. She strikes me as the type who might sue."

Scott pulled a face. "Would you believe we've got to make sure the sleigh is fitted with effing sleigh bells? That's the latest directive from on high."

"Ssh." Holly poked Scott in the side. "Don't listen to Mr Scrooge here. If the customer wants us to bling up the Christmas element, who are we to argue?"

"Oh really?" Scott narrowed his eyes, but they glinted with amusement. "Only last night you were saying if she made you paint one of the reindeers' noses red like Rudolf you'd stick the paint brush where the...oof."

Holly poked Scott even harder in the stomach this time and rolled her eyes at Amy.

"Oh," Amy shifted the bag on her shoulder, fiddling with the straps and feeling awkward. "Did you need me? I could help you later on before dinner?"

She felt traitorous, on her way to wreck the very event Holly was stressing over.

"It's kind of you to offer, Amy," Scott smiled at her as he wound his arms around Holly. "But there's no need, this is your free time after all and she's already got me roped in making table decorations."

The way Scott looked at Holly, eyes brimming with affection and an intimacy reflected in Holly's eyes too.

I had that once…

Holly waved her away. "Go and have fun, it'll all work out okay."

I do hope so, I really do hope so.

It wasn't hard to find Juliet's group. Amy heard them first, talking loudly and disturbing the peace of the spa. She spotted them sitting in a circle around the jacuzzi, their legs dangling into the bubbling water. There was a gap, if she sat with her headphones in hopefully they'd think she was listening to music and if they saw her fiddling with her phone think she was scrolling through her playlist. If she kept her iPhone in the waterproof case it should be okay.

She slipped into the gap; glad the other women barely glanced at her. Just as she'd thought, they didn't appear to recognise her.

Invisible.

She surreptitiously set her phone to voice record, knowing it could easily record for several hours. As the women chatted about people she'd never heard of Amy found her attention drifting off, Josh's words reverberating inside her head.

She'd never believed that stuff about him ending their relationship for her sake at the time. Back at twenty-one she would've bitten someone's head off if they'd told her she was too young to marry. But now…well she could see it was true, they had been too young to marry. And she had been psyched about teaching. Could she really have coped with being marooned in an ex-pat compound with nothing better to do with her time than top up her tan?

Had he been right to leave her to follow her own dreams? Maybe…

She squeezed her eyes shut briefly. It all made sense in her head, but her heart refused to agree. Josh had set her free but she hadn't wanted her freedom, she'd wanted him. The more she thought about it, her anger with Josh seeped away to be replaced by a terrible sadness.

It felt like such a terrible waste and she couldn't let Josh make another mistake in the name of "doing the right thing". This wasn't about whatever she imagined might happen between her and Josh. This was about protecting Josh from Juliet because he was far too nice to see what a cow she really was.

Amy had tuned out the conversation but her Josh-antennae twitched when the conversation turned round to the wedding. She tried not to look interested, fixing her gaze on the darkened glass window with its view of the mountain tops.

"So he rang you last night?" The brunette with a Cleopatra bob asked her. "I thought you'd agreed no contact between stags and hens?"

"Do you think he's got cold feet?" A woman with expensive-looking highlights raised a perfectly plucked eyebrow.

"If he has I've got a little trick up my sleeve." Juliet stared at her friend, her face impassive. "I haven't spent months getting myself in shape for this wedding for nothing. Not to mention the stress of dealing with that inept wedding planner. And I've got more relatives and friends flying into Geneva tomorrow. Do you think I'd let myself be jilted and humiliated in front of them?"

Amy's stomach clenched, but she kept her eyes fixed on a mountain top and tried to look bored. It was difficult when she wanted to leap up and slap Juliet.

"Can you imagine the humiliation of being jilted?" Ms Blonde Highlights replied, a cruel twist at the edge of her mouth when she smiled.

"But I can't imagine Josh jilting you, he's too decent." Ms Cleopatra Bob butted in. "And this ski wedding was his idea wasn't it?"

"Yes," Juliet replied. "He said he didn't want to do the traditional thing or his parents not being there would be too awful. I don't mind, after all you've got to admit it's different."

Please someone ask her what trick she has up her sleeve Amy pleaded silently, her muscles tense as she waited. She had a nagging feeling about this "trick", she needed to know.

"Do you remember Tara?" Cleopatra bob girl asked in the hushed tones of someone about to enjoy some juicy gossip. "When she was jilted, she lost it big time. I think they had to cart her off to the Priory."

"There's no way I'd let anyone humiliate me like that," Juliet's voice had a hard edge to it.

"So, what's your trick then? If it turns out he's got cold feet?" Bob girl asked. "Not that he will, though. How could he not be really into you?"

Halleluiah. At last someone has asked the question.

But Amy's exhilaration was tinged with trepidation. She had a very bad feeling about this.

"I'll tell him I'm pregnant of course." Juliet replied, sounding smug. "As you said, Josh is a decent guy, quite old fashioned when it comes to that sort of thing."

The involuntary gasp had escaped Amy's mouth before she could stop it. Rage erupted inside her as she swung her legs out of the Jacuzzi, getting ready to stand up, unable to bear being so close to Juliet for one minute longer.

"Hey, isn't that the weird girl from the wedding planners?" Ms Blonde Highlights announced loudly and the rest of the group stared at Amy. Juliet's eyes narrowed.

"Why aren't you working on my wedding?" Juliet demanded icily, glaring at Amy as though she had no right to use the same facilities as her.

"It's not really my job, and I er…had today off." Amy pulled her headphones out of her ears and got to her feet, in her haste she knocked the screen lock button and the iPhone fell down onto the blue-tiled floor.

Oh crap.

The voice-recording app was visible on the screen.

"You're recording me?" Juliet's voice rose, fury blazing in her eyes as she made a lunge for the phone and picked it up.

Amy wasn't quick enough to get there first and Juliet's friends stood up to block her from reaching Juliet.

"I could click erase, but maybe I should make sure." Juliet pulled the phone out of the waterproof case and threw it into the air above the. Unable to move forward Amy could only watch as it fell into the middle of the bubbling Jacuzzi. The rage inside her was bubbling too, threatening to boil over.

"Oops, sorry, looks like your phone is fucked." Juliet sneered. "I guess that's one of the hazards of recording people without their permission. Now why don't you tell me why you were spying on me because I'd say it's not just your phone that's in trouble."

Josh sat in the sun outside the Chalet Repos. A morning's skiing hadn't helped him sort his mind out. The conversation with Juliet last night had made him less and less sure he could go through with this. How could he ever have thought she was the right one to settle down with? What had he been thinking? That you should just marry whoever you were with when the music stopped?

Grief had made him settle for the wrong person – right place, right time, wrong girl.

Juliet was the poor man's Amy. No, scratch that, she didn't compare at all. There'd been a tone in her voice last night he didn't like and didn't recognise. How well did he really know Juliet?

He'd rushed into this. Losing his parents left him longing to create his own family. Juliet had been there at the right place, right time. She was good company and energetic in bed. Also she'd said she loved to travel and was happy to up and relocate if he took another job abroad.

He'd thought it was worth settling to start a family. You didn't get two people like Amy in one lifetime. If only he'd known that… But he'd stuffed up and had to live with the consequences. Or did he?

He'd come back to the chalet early in the hope he might be

able to find Amy again and talk to her; the other girls had said she wasn't skiing today. But there'd been no sign of her at Chalet Repos.

He could hear the iPod dock playing Christmas songs on a loop from inside the chalet, now on was *All I want for Christmas...*

And he knew all he wanted for Christmas was Amy. There was no point fighting the truth. The question was what should he do about it? He kicked hard at the fresh powdery snow on the ground. Had Amy been telling him the truth about Juliet?

Yes.

His gut had no doubt. Juliet had been weird with him on the phone, her answers about Ibiza snappy. There was nothing he could put his finger on. Just a feeling, a difference in the tone of her voice, a barrier between them.

No evidence in other words. Nothing of substance to give him cause to call off a wedding, to disrupt the travel plans of their friends and family. It should be a no-brainer. So why couldn't he accept that?

He stared at the road leading up to the chalet. He must be hallucinating because he could've sworn that was Juliet and Amy walking together towards Chalet Repos.

What the...

Josh sat up straighter, peering forwards. No, he wasn't hallucinating.

He got to his feet. As they got closer he saw the furious look on Juliet's face, her skin mottled crimson with fury. He turned his gaze on Amy, her eyes were puffy and red, he could see that even from this distance.

What on earth had happened? How....

Juliet marched up to the chalet, Amy doggedly trailing a few steps behind her. A spark in Amy's eyes, of pride and determination, moved him.

He crushed the instinct to go to Amy and wrap his arms around her. He had to play fair by Juliet.

"If you'll excuse me," Juliet turned to Amy, her words laced with sarcasm. "I want to talk to *my* fiancé and Mrs Hamilton about your shocking behaviour."

Amy met Josh's gaze, cheeks flushed and eyes wide and pleading.

"If I were you I'd start checking the flights back to the UK." Juliet practically spat out the words. "Because you won't have a job by the end of the day. Good luck with that, I hear Christmas Eve is a bitch of a day to travel. I'd like to help you, but I've got a wedding to prepare for."

"Holly isn't here," Josh said, his eyes scanning Amy's face, flushed pink, crimson spots burning in her cheeks. He knew that look; she was furious, equally as furious as Juliet, but containing it, just about.

"What exactly is the matter?" Josh added, perplexed. What on earth had Amy done to make Juliet so angry? Instinctively he wanted to protect her. "Shall we sit down and talk about this like adults?"

Juliet snorted. Amy ignored her and walked over to a deckchair close to Josh, slumping gratefully down into it, ignoring the narky glare cast her way by Juliet.

Amy turned towards Josh, hands clasped tightly in her lap.

"I got you your proof," she said calmly. "I got you the evidence that you shouldn't marry her."

"You little..." Juliet surged forward towards Amy, hand raised. Josh blocked Juliet's arm and grasped it firmly. She glared at him. "So, how long have you been having an affair with that piece of..."

"I haven't," Josh cut in calmly, although he felt anything but calm.

Juliet snorted again. "Why else would she be creeping around and trying to record my private conversations? You must think I'm an idiot."

"We used to be an item, at university. Amy is just looking out for me. What's all this talk about evidence? Evidence of what?"

If he had evidence of an affair, no one could blame him for calling everything off, surely? What should he do?

Call off the wedding, find out what's up with Amy, really talk to her and find out if things can be rekindled.

His heart was quite sure of what he wanted to do. But calling off the wedding would be a big move. What if this was simply a case of classic cold feet?

It's not, you know it's not.

"Show him your evidence then," Juliet sneered, trying to jerk her arm out of Josh's grip. "Don't worry, I'm not going to hurt your girlfriend. How touching of you to defend her."

He let go and turned his gaze to Amy. She stared up at him from her deckchair, her fingers interlaced tightly, her eyes wide and pleading.

"I don't have it. Juliet dropped my phone in the Jacuzzi," Amy admitted. "I think it's pretty much had it. Maybe it will dry out, but I doubt it."

Juliet smiled smugly. "She shouldn't record people without their knowledge. I wonder what the privacy law is in Switzerland. I'm pretty sure it's illegal. I could get her into a whole lot of trouble."

"Come on Juliet, let's not make this even worse than it already is. Let's have a bit of dignity, okay?" Josh replied, flashing her an angry look.

"I'm sorry Josh darling," Juliet's voice became wheedling. "It's just all been so unbelievably stressful, trying to tie up all the wedding loose ends and then having your deranged ex-girlfriend stalking me. If you say nothing has happened between the two of you, I'll believe you."

Juliet had pulled out a tissue and was dabbing delicately at her eyes. "It's all been so emotional. I was going to wait until our wedding day to tell you but I may as well…I'm pregnant Josh, isn't that amazing?"

Josh felt like he'd been punched. He stared at Juliet, momentarily stunned by her change of tack. She believed *him* that nothing had been going on. God, she was good at turning the tables.

What if she really was pregnant, though? Although nothing

was ever one hundred per cent effective, it still seemed unlikely, considering how careful he was. Could Juliet really be pregnant?

"She's lying." Amy jumped to her feet, her small hands curled into fists. "Josh, she's lying, don't listen to her."

"Amy, I think I need to talk to Juliet alone. Could you leave us for a minute?" Josh stared at Juliet, suddenly filled with absolute certainty.

He knew what he had to do.

Amy staggered back as though he'd slapped her, her face draining of colour, turning almost as white as the snow surrounding them. He wanted to reach out and reassure her, but he had to do this properly. She turned and walked stiffly to the chalet entrance.

"You heard him," Juliet smirked as she called out after Amy. "And don't think you've heard the last of this. I'll be having words with Mrs Hamilton. I'm not having you anywhere near *my* wedding."

Once Amy was inside the chalet Josh turned his gaze onto Juliet. Her eyes had a malicious gleam to them, like a cat about to play with a captured mouse. She thought she'd won.

"There isn't going to be a wedding, Juliet," he spoke as kindly as he could manage, after all, they were both at fault here. He shouldn't have rushed things when he barely knew her.

"Are you serious?" Juliet screeched. "You're taking the word of that little… slut?"

"No, Juliet." It became harder to control his voice, but he kept it low. This was going to be hard for her to deal with, after all Juliet really cared about what people thought. "We should never had got engaged, it was all too quick and we barely know each other, as I think today has shown. Can we talk about this like adults, rather than resorting to a slanging match?"

She glowered at him. "You're really calling it off?"

"There is no baby, is there Juliet?" He stared her down.

"Fuck you, Josh," Juliet hissed then turned around and stomped off back towards the hotel.

Josh watched her, thinking it was odd how little he cared. Juliet could blacken his name, say she'd ended it because he was sleeping with Amy and tell all kinds of lies and he didn't give a monkeys.

Now he needed to find Amy.

CHAPTER SEVEN

Amy stumbled into the dorm room. At first she was glad the girls were out skiing, but then she found herself wishing for a pair of arms to comfort her.

So. That's that then.

She'd done her best and the now the fight had drained out of her. That Juliet would lie about being pregnant shouldn't have surprised her, but it felt like a knife being twisted in her guts; she felt an actual physical pain in her stomach. She slumped down onto the floor beneath the window, drawing her knees up to her chest, vaguely aware of the tears streaming down her cheeks.

This wasn't fair. But then life wasn't, she already knew that. She'd have to suck it up.

And she would, once she'd worked out how to scrape herself up off the floor. Just as she'd clawed her way up out of the depression, getting better and better at hiding her sadness away from the world in general and her family in particular. She never wanted to put her parents through the stress of her illness again.

And now she'd have to find storage space for this pain too, find a way of containing it. She'd just have to work harder, run quicker and ski faster to keep the dark clouds at bay. Because she couldn't go back to those bleak depression days with her parents faces creased with concern and the tablets that made her feel zombie-ish and decidedly un-her. She hadn't liked taking them. It seemed pointless, after all you couldn't take a pill to cure a broken heart or bring the dead back to life. She hadn't wanted to pretend everything was okay because it bloody well wasn't.

But over time she had to pretend, just to get everyone off her back. She'd missed a good chunk of the start of term for teacher training. They said she could defer her place a year, but somehow she'd never wanted to go back. All the excitement about a career as a primary school teacher had been drained out of her. She'd also lost her confidence; how could she be in charge of small children if some days she could barely bring herself to shower?

The only way to keep depression at bay was to keep moving from job to job, relationship to relationship and even country to country. That had been particularly effective. Pretending and continually moving had been for her own sake too.

But now she wanted to press the pause button on it all. She needed to stop.

But she might've known that excavating the past would lead to this – crouching in a room, crying her eyes out, feeling lonelier than she'd ever felt before.

There was a knock on the door. Amy looked up, startled. The girls wouldn't bother to knock and Holly wouldn't be back until dinnertime.

"Ye…es?" she croaked, wondering if Juliet had come in to have another go at her. What if Juliet did get Amy thrown out? Given what she'd done to one of Holly's clients, Amy had to be prepared. How much money did she have – enough to find accommodation on Christmas Eve in Verbier if she couldn't get a flight?

Not a chance. She'd be reduced to begging for a space on someone's floor or even worse, trying to find a hook-up for the night. She shuddered.

The door opened to reveal Josh, looking like a giant in the tiny room.

"Hi," he said, warm brown eyes fixed on her. She wanted to

drink him in, hit some sense into him and make love to him all at once. Confused just didn't cover it.

"Hi," she whispered back, hiccupping. Her hands trembled, so she linked them around her knees, pulling them up towards her chest.

Unspoken questions hung in the air, emotional vibrations making the atmosphere heavy with tension. Amy wanted to scream.

How can it be "the right thing" to give Ms Bridezilla the benefit of the doubt but not to trust me, not to be there for me? What about doing the right thing by me, Josh?

She opened her mouth, but the words seemed to stick in her throat.

"How could you believe her?" she asked, feeling raw and exposed.

"I don't." Josh said, coming into the room and closing the door behind him. He got down onto the floor beside her.

"Oh?" It felt like she'd stepped into a lift, only to find herself falling down the shaft. Her heart beat wildly, hope, fear and desire pulsing through her.

He sat, his back against the wall, his body pressed up against hers, the warmth comforting her.

"I believe you Amy. And I was marrying Juliet for all the wrong reasons. I barely knew her. But it felt like the right time to marry, to make a family, create some ties…"

"Did you love her?" Amy broke in, letting her head fall to rest on his shoulder. The warmth from the underfloor heating thawed her out.

Where do we go from here?

"I persuaded myself I did, but then I was in a bad place, after mum and dad, you know…" There was a catch in his voice and Amy reached over instinctively, taking one of his hands in hers and squeezing it.

"Is it off then? The wedding, I mean." Amy's heart seemed to leap up into her throat as she waited for Josh's answer.

"Yes, definitely off." He spoke decisively.

"Holly's going to kill me." Amy nestled her head closer into Josh's shoulder. Even if this left her jobless and homeless she didn't regret a thing. The vice-like grip around her chest loosened its grip and she could breathe easily again.

Her skin prickled with anticipation as he stroked the palm of her hand with his thumb, slowly, suggestively. Every hormone in her body screamed at her to throw away her objections, to let go of the pain and fear he might hurt her again.

To forgive him.

He hadn't meant to be callous, she could see that now. He was a good man. What had happened had just been one of those things.

Josh bent his head down towards her, lips parted as though about to kiss her.

"I was depressed," she blurted out before his lips could reach hers.

He paused and stared. "What?"

"I became clinically depressed after you left for your job in Saudi, that's why I'm not teaching, why I didn't go to teacher-training college." She stared down at their hands, still linked tightly together. "Grandad died of a heart attack, and that combined with you…well they think it triggered it. A reactive depression."

"Why on earth didn't you tell me?" He frowned, pulling her closer.

She shrugged. "What was the point? We weren't in touch and you didn't want to be. It didn't change anything."

She looked up at him, tears rolling down her face and dripping off her chin. He lifted a hand and, with his thumb, gently wiped the tears away. Then his mouth followed where his thumb had touched her and he kissed her tears away, so tenderly she felt the hard lump of ice around her heart begin to melt.

Where had this tenderness been when she needed it? She shuddered, all questions receding as his lips trailed kisses down to her neck and he nuzzled her. Slowly the tears stopped falling and she let herself enjoy what he was doing to her.

"I'm so sorry I wasn't there for you Amy," he said softly. "I wish I'd known. I really never meant to hurt you, I just thought it was the right thing to do, for both of us…"

"Ssh." She put one finger on his lips, she needed his kisses more than his words right now. "Let's put it behind us, I've had enough of being miserable, I want to say hello properly."

She trailed one hand over his chest, suggestively, tentatively, asking him with her eyes, wanting so much to be one with him again her body ached. She felt sick of thinking about sad stuff. Enough. She wanted to live, to enjoy life.

She wanted to make love to Josh.

Josh smiled at her, the gleam in his eye telling her all she needed to know. They were always good at reading one another's bodies. She climbed into his lap, straddling him, her mouth meeting his with a hunger that took her breath away. She pressed down onto his hard thighs and his growing erection.

Josh pulled her harder up against him, wrapping her in his arms, his mouth moving onto her neck and his hands moving up inside her top, pulling it up over her head. He lowered his mouth to her breasts, softly kissing each nipple through the fabric of her bra.

She pressed more urgently against him, desperate for all clothing barriers to be pushed away, to feel skin on skin with Josh again. This felt so long overdue, every frustration, every dream about him combining to make her sizzle with sexual tension. Her skin felt super-sensitised, she jerked beneath his kisses, as though he were charging her with each kiss, slowly bringing her back to life again.

She was finished with living life on her reserve battery, she wanted to feel fully alive again, to let herself feel.

Pulling at his long-sleeved t-shirt with one hand she lowered the other hand to tug at the button fly of his jeans. Frantically they pulled and tugged at clothing until they were finally naked except for Amy's underwear, discarded clothes lying on the floor around them. They stood breathing hard, staring, remembering, wanting…

"Take off your knickers." The sexy grin she remembered so well was back on Josh's face. "You won't be needed them."

Her insides went into free-fall again, as she slipped her fingers into the knicker elastic and edged them down her thighs, eventually stepping out of them. She unclasped her bra and threw it up onto her bunk, drinking in the appreciative gleam in Josh's eyes.

"I've missed you," she whispered.

"Me too." Josh stared back, eyes dark with desire. "What do you say, do we give it another go?"

She gazed down at his erection and raised an eyebrow. "I think we should."

Seized by a desire to be as intimately close to Josh as possible she knelt down, taking his erection in her mouth. He groaned as her mouth formed a tight ring around him and her tongue darted out to lick and tease him. When he'd stiffened even more, she knew she needed him inside her, wanting to be truly reunited.

She stood up again, kissing and licking up to his chest to his nipples and neck, every bit of flesh she could reach. Wanting to finally believe this might be true, to drink him in and to make them one again.

Josh put a hand on her shoulder. "Turn around, it's your turn."

He bent her over the bunk bed, his hands stroking inside her thighs as he pulled her legs apart to position her. She shuddered as his fingers slipped up inside her and dipped in and out, rubbing her clit. He'd always been good at this and he knew exactly what she liked, knew this was her favourite position as he could thrust more deeply.

She moaned and writhed against his hand, loving what he was doing but needing him inside her. She could feel him pressed up against her and felt deliciously exposed. He teased her into a delicious release, her orgasm rocking her body, piercing her in two before sending her floating. But still she ached for him inside her, she felt empty.

"I need you inside me now," she begged. "I'm, um… on the pill so…no need for, um…"

She hoped he couldn't see her flushed face, but she had to tell him, wanted so much to feel him inside her without the barrier of a condom.

"Okay," Josh whispered.

Josh stood back and pulled her legs even further apart, exposing her to him. She felt the cool air against her sex. He must be able to see how wet she was for him but she felt no embarrassment, she felt totally comfortable and very, very turned on.

Amy's breasts ached, pressed hard into the mattress. She was ready for him, oh so ready.

"Please," she begged again as he rubbed the tip of his erection against her sex, spreading the wetness.

Then he plunged inside her, deep and hard, making her gasp. This had always been their favourite position, the thrusts so much deeper. She met each of his thrusts and once they found their rhythm they moved in time, a hot molten wetness swelling inside her.

"Amy," Josh groaned as he jerked inside her, shuddering as he rode the wave of his own orgasm. She rode it with him, coming together.

They both slid to the floor and Amy climbed onto his lap, sitting sideways, arms around his neck.

"Where do we go from here Amy?" He planted a soft kiss on the top of her head.

"I don't know," she replied, her head resting against his chest, listening to the reassuring sound of his heartbeat. Thud, thud, thud… "But I hope we can work something out. I don't want to be apart from you again."

"Me neither," Josh agreed. "I'm going to find some accommodation here in Verbier for the New Year. How long are you contracted here for?"

"Just until February half-term time. Then I've got nothing

planned. Well unless Holly fires me, that is." Amy exhaled slowly; could she summon any sympathy for Juliet?

It was a stretch.

Although she did feel some guilt at the chaos she'd caused, she suspected she'd get over it. There were consolations. She nestled against Josh, feeling the tension seeping away.

"They're always looking for classroom assistants at the British and American schools in the Middle East and there are lots of job opportunities out there for engineers. There's one I'd like to go for in Oman, it's very different to Saudi. You'd be able to work and drive and we could go to the beach or wadi bashing in the desert. Would you like that? We could always stay in the UK if you'd like, only I don't feel ready to go back to Exmoor."

"I understand," she replied, finding his hand and squeezing it. "And I think that sounds like fun."

"So." Scott looked quizzically down the table at Amy and Josh. "We're not having the wedding today then; it's all off?"

"No." Josh shook his head. "No wedding. But as we've already bought the food and drink and your lovely wife has put so much effort into the planning, I thought we could turn the reception into a Christmas Eve party. I think we all could do with a bit of chilling out."

He had wondered about seeing if he could marry Amy today instead, but there wasn't enough time to sort out the legalities, and anyway, it was too soon.

Holly smiled weakly. "Amen to that." She looked pointedly at Amy. "When you said you were willing to help out I had no idea you were planning to take the whole event off my hands."

There was humour in her tone, though.

Amy smiled wryly. "Sorry about that. But I sort of had to, sometimes you just know, don't you?"

"Yes," Holly replied softly. "You do."

"So, we're all on for a party tonight, then?" Tash whooped,

breaking the moment.

They all got up from the table, Amy visibly relieved at not being sacked.

Josh pulled Amy aside. "I told you Scott and Holly would be cool with it, they've been paid, after all and I got the impression Holly and Juliet didn't hit it off."

"Yes," Amy smiled the smile that Josh had been missing since they day she'd dropped the cake. It was a cheeky smile, mischievous and full of life.

"Come over to the Christmas tree," he murmured in her ear. "I've got a present for you."

She grinned, the smile transforming her heart-shaped face. "But shouldn't we wait for Christmas day?"

"I found something I knew you'd love at the Christmas market." He reached up to a small silver parcel tied onto the tree. "Didn't you know they give presents on Christmas Eve in Switzerland? When in Verbier…"

She took the present, kissing him lightly on the mouth, and he marvelled that he could reach out and touch her whenever she wanted. Finally. After the initial fuss had died down yesterday and Holly had managed to dispatch Juliet, everyone had turned a blind eye to Amy moving into Josh's room.

Opening the present she gasped. "You remembered?"

In her hand lay an exquisite platinum hare pendant.

"Of course. Do you still have the brooch I gave you?"

She nodded. "Would you put the pendant on for me?"

She held up her hair and he fastened the pendant around her neck. He hoped the bounce would gradually reappear into Amy's life. One thing he knew, he was certainly never letting her go again.

"But I feel bad now, I haven't got anything to give you." Amy protested.

"Oh yes you have." Josh pulled her into his arms, smiling down at her.

The tree glittered behind them and the Michael Buble version of the song he'd heard yesterday came onto the iPod dock. *All I want for Christmas…*

Is you.

How had he managed to get things so wrong? Now he'd made the decision to call off the wedding and to be with Amy both his heart and mind were filled with an overwhelming peace. He'd been so obsessed with what was right and wrong he'd missed what was right under his nose. Next time he was listening to his gut.

"All I want for Christmas is you," he sang along to the music, manoeuvring Amy beneath the mistletoe Tash had pinned to the beam. Holding her tightly he stopped singing to kiss her, then he pulled away and whispered into her ear, "All I want for Christmas is you, Amy."

Tash wolf-whistled from the doorway. "At last. You two took your time."

Amy stuck her tongue out at Tash.

"I've just got one question for Josh," Tash declared sternly, a hand on each hip.

Amy stirred uneasily in Josh's arms. He guessed she was wondering how long it would take to cross the room and rugby tackle Tash to the ground.

He stroked Amy's hip reassuringly and met Tash's sharp eyes. "Go ahead."

Tash raised an eyebrow. "What *are* you going to do with the sodding reindeer?"

www.ingramcontent.com/pod-product-compliance
Lightning Source LLC
Chambersburg PA
CBHW010644100726
47900CB00011B/2963